Scott Langston is currently living in Thailand where he is, amongst other things, a husband, a father and a teacher. In respect of the latter, he wishes to disassociate himself utterly and unconditionally from the central character of this novel.

In his increasingly rare spare time, he writes increasingly less often. He is working on this.

To those who dare to love.

I am so powerful,
I love so much,
I feel infinity.
Without me, nothing exists.
I am love, and so are you.

the alpha to omega

Scott Langston

www.scottlangston.org

part one

the alpha

Tuesday 15th August

I have broken free! I feel like a character from "The Great Escape"; I can hear the theme tune in my head, see the steely grimace on McQueen's face. I feel like breaking into a run, clicking my heels together, Andy Capp style. The sheer exhilaration of it! Was I so fed up with England that I feel this elated to be free of it? Apparently so. As the taxi pulled up to my new apartment, Rachel shouted down to ask, in Greek, how much it was. The taxi driver promptly reduced his fare by almost half, dumped my bags brusquely on the street and took my money most ungraciously before slamming his door after him and speeding off, tyres squealing as he went. Welcome to Greece.

Five minutes later, re-united with Rachel and Richard, I was sat on a balcony in 32 degrees of Mediterranean sunshine, drinking gin and tonic with a slice of lemon, memories of a cold and damp northern England already faded. Yes! I think I'm going to like it here.

Later, in the privacy of my own room, I am assailed by the enormity of what I have done. I have always believed that a few short hours, minutes or seconds even, given the right circumstances, can change your life. Here I am, my life changed! I look out of the French windows, wondering vaguely why they are called that, and see mountains in the near distance. The cloudless sky is a brilliant blue. The heat is oppressive, but feels good nonetheless. I feel inspired. I feel alive.

> *What limits the 'is'?*
> *Fear*
> *Take heart*
> *Take a deep breath*

Boldly step forward
Into your life.
Only you can do this
Only you can create regrets
For decisions not made
Chances not taken.
Only you can be true enough
To yourself
To allow yourself
To live.

I have this slightly uncomfortable feeling that I have come here to run away. Bollocks to it. What's wrong with running away? "He who fights and runs away..."

I throw my backpack onto the double bed. I met a guy in a pub in north London only two days ago who used to live here. Not randomly, I might add – we did arrange to meet. I paid him seventy-five quid for the furniture he left behind: a double bed, matching desk and distinctly weird-looking hat stand. Not bad, I think, now that I see them. I need to sit down and breathe deeply and resist the temptation to giggle like a child. I have stepped out of my predictable life in England; stepped away from an impending marriage, from kids too-soon-to-be-able-to-offer-them-anything, from mortgages and debts, from the future I was following, my pre-ordained Hell. My future is no longer the claustrophobic place I don't want to visit; it's wide open, full of uncertainty and possibilities I can't yet see. I like this feeling. That is ever-so slightly understated.

I can't face unpacking just yet, so I shall wander downstairs to where I hear ice cubes clinking invitingly...

Wednesday 16th August

I have pinched myself. Several times. It is true. I have only a minor hangover to deal with now before hitting the sun.

Shit, it's bright out there! I'll do some tentative unpacking instead. My Greek-God-like tan can wait a couple of days.

Thursday 17th August

I am still living out of my bag, and feeling as though I am on holiday. It's as though unpacking would make all of this seem too real. I am still enjoying the dream of it! I'm sharing this apartment with Rachel, an

Australian girl who works in a nearby nursery, and two other girls who are going to be doing some kind of media work. They're not here yet, so we have this huge rambling apartment to ourselves.

Friday 18th August

My first sojourn into school. I have an unbelievable amount of work to do! The order for resources which I placed in April is apparently held up in Greek customs and unlikely to arrive before September. Allegedly, it's being stalled in anticipation of some kind of a bribe. This does not bode well. Am I in the Third World here? After all my hard work here last April, we'll still be starting a new term with fifty children aged four and five on borrowed equipment and resources. Indeed this does not bode well. Also, now that I've arrived, the Head's previous good humour and camaraderie seems strangely absent. My contract hasn't started yet and I feel definite warning tremors.

Dad's birthday. I must phone him. I must remember not to gloat about the weather and life in general. Damn, this is a good feeling!

Spent the day drinking *frappé* coffees by the pool. Oh yes, the pool. Also, squash courts, a pretty good climbing wall and a fully equipped gym. In my head, I am drafting letters home to friends: I must remember to gloat.

Letters home: a strange sensation as I write that word. Where's home now?

Supposedly there's unpacking and sorting out to do in the classroom, but as I have nothing to unpack or sort out... Anyway, it's Friday. After a hard week's work, I'm looking forward to a relaxing weekend.

Saturday 19th August

I took a day off from my hectic preparations, well, ok, my lethargic and procastinatory preparations (if such an adjective exists) and went into Plaka in central Athens. I took the metro for the first time. It was very cheap, very busy and very hot. Got off the train at Monastiraki, which is the nearest stop to the Acropolis. I'm saving that visit for another time, content for now to roam the backstreets. Very touristy. Very hot. Very short visit. Resisted the mild temptation to buy someone a "My friend went to Athens and all I got was this lousy T-shirt" T-shirt, and sent postcards instead. Sat briefly watching the scantily clad Greek women strutting to and fro - a welcome change from duffel-coated Northerners. Spent the return train journey fantasizing happily about them - the scantily clad Greek women, not the duffel-coated Northerners.

Got back to find Rachel preparing a barbecue, so joined in the work - tasting the humus, lighting the charcoal, pouring the gin and tonics. It's a dirty job, but someone has to do it. Noticed for the first time that Rachel is way up there in the scantily-clad Greeks league, though not Greek. Interesting.

I tell myself 'NO', however, in loud capital letters, as part of the plan in coming to Greece is to keep away from complicated or otherwise potentially serious liaisons. My resolve is strong so far and I am only slightly worried by the fact that we spend much time together drinking large amounts of gin.

Too much sun and far too much gin, however diluted with tonic it may be, do not mix well. Retired somewhat inelegantly after the view through the open windows started to spin slowly. I shattered the collected glasses on a small coffee table rather impressively as I stood and made my wordless way to bed.

Cannot believe that I will ever settle down to work in this country.

Monday 21st August

I spent Sunday in bed/on the couch being administered various odd-looking 'sure-thing' hangover cures. Rachel was very concerned. I was torn between liking the attention and frankly wishing that she wasn't so charmingly attentive. We finally ventured out in the evening to a nearby *taverna* to sample the wonders of Greek vegetarian cooking. Actually I was very impressed - a spinach-like salad, a fried white cheese and some cheese-bally type thingies. Great!

I also tentatively discovered *retsina*. It's harsh at first but soon settles down into something I think I could get to quite like. It's also extremely cheap. However, I was determined to go to bed sober one night before this course of action was actually required for me by the notion of work the following day. Hangovers and small children... don't go there! During the course of the evening I also met an interesting Danish woman who seemed keen to practise her English. Or maybe just seemed keen. Oh, what a cosmopolitan existence I have all of a sudden!

Met more colleagues from the Primary Section today in school. Very friendly, some ingratiatingly so. Others genuinely interested and trying to help me settle in. I seem to have been sold to them by the Head as some sort of genius set to inspire great change. Am trying to down-shift in teaching, but suspect I will not be able to. This is a worrying development. Also, there seems to be a huge Primary/Secondary divide, both professionally and socially. We are viewed as second class citizens in the grand hierarchy. One Secondary English teacher actually asked me if I enjoyed babysitting. This is also worrying.

Tuesday 22nd August

Down-shifting is definitely not an option. I am clearly going to be expected to work for the money they are paying me. Interestingly enough, the money they said they would be paying me is not actually the money they will be paying me. I figure I've been sold short by about nine hundred quid a year. The bursar doesn't seem to understand my protestations, assuring me that, "This is a very good wage for Greece." Is it me, or is that not the point? They seem to think that because they are paying me a lot, they don't need to pay me what they promised back in England. Am increasingly worried by this state of affairs, but am told not to worry as 'this is Greece'. Mentioned to the Head that I'd like a written contract soonish; before I actually started work, for example. She gave me a look which suggested I had implied her to be a liar and a cheat. Somewhere we have got off on the wrong foot, but I'm not sure where or when that happened. A number of colleagues have made non-too-subtle queries about what I am being paid. Surely this kind of stuff is published and out in the open? I think I have not been told quite everything in this scenario.

Wednesday 23rd August

I spent last night with Richard, a fellow inmate; from about nine until four this morning, we sat in a pizza restaurant steadily drinking magically replenishing bottles of ice-cold Amstel beer. Rachel was due to show up but didn't. I learnt that her recent long term boyfriend has finished with her. Have to admit that a selfish 'Oh good' response surfaced in my brain slightly ahead of more appropriate thoughts of concern. Didn't admit this however, and went with the latter for the sake of form.

Predictably enough, the evening drifted into incoherent drunken ramblings about failed romances and embellished personal anecdotes. The potted history of many of the people I have met out here so far seems to involve escape from the past. As my escape was from the future, I decided to remain non-committal for the time being. Seems I am definitely not the only one here seeking refuge.

Played a scratch card lotto game and won ten thousand drachmas, about twelve quid. However, drank a lot more than this.

Thursday 24th August

Rachel was very apologetic for not having showed last night. She had a quiet night in with a girlfriend who turns out to be the previously met interesting Danish woman, with the very Danish-sounding name of Trudy. Interesting is also interested, apparently, in me. There ensues a difficult conversation in which I try to keep all my options open. Try to show enough interest in Trudy for the news to get back to her, and also appear distracted enough to stir up interest in Rachel. Old habits die hard. My "I don't want to get involved with anyone" line catches her attention, especially as I refuse to embellish upon it. This tactic receives friendly squeeze of hand and dazzling smile which combine to make me feel cheap. What am I doing? I seriously do not want to get involved with this woman. Well, my head doesn't. She wants to go into Athens tomorrow night and do I want to go with her? Do I really want to get into the 'sympathising-for-loss-of-boyfriend' stuff? I am not going to take advantage of anyone's vulnerability. At least, I think I'm not.

School beckoned again, but only for a few hours. There was a most impressive downpour of torrential rain for a while, just as I was walking in. This was especially fun as the lack of pavements and of drainage combine to turn the roads into mini white-water rapids, which passing motorists only too happily spray liberally over pedestrians. Actually, pedestrian, singular. Me. I noticed that nobody else was daft enough to be walking around in this weather. We live and learn.

The beauty of 36 degrees, however, is that I was dry in an hour and sipping Amstel by the pool in the company of like-minded colleagues.

I also now have a classroom which is beginning to look something like a classroom ought to look.

Friday 25th August

As I am obliged to go into work from next Thursday, I decide to take a break for a long weekend. Following this logic, I'm not going into school today. Rachel is spending the day with interesting Danish woman but will be back for our excursion into Athens by seven this evening.

For the first time since I arrived, I spend almost an entire day by myself. I unpack properly. I experiment with Greek T.V. As far as I can make out, there are twelve different channels, all dedicated to adverts. Every now and then, a few minutes of an actual programme, then lots more adverts. Many adverts are repeated twice in the same programme break. Interesting concept. I watched "Knight Rider," "SeaQuest DSV" and "Mission Impossible". Sad, I know.

My first jaunt to a supermarket! I came away with lots of spaghetti and tinned tomatoes, cheese, milk and bread. Oh, and supplies of alcohol for the weekend. There was a grand total of absolutely no pre-packed Vegetarian meals. I know, I counted twice. I'm actually going to have to cook! Rachel, I noticed, has a sandwich toaster, so no crisis just yet.

At around six, I started to make movements in the kitchen. Rachel arrived early, kicked me out onto the balcony with a cold beer and announced that she was cooking. Richard arrived from where he had supposedly been working at school. The beer he rescued from the fridge was clearly not his first, so I suspect I am not the only one who finds the pool an irresistible lure from nobler activities.

Sunday 27th August

Our new flatmates are both due to arrive sometime today - I wonder what it will be like sharing a house with three girls. Not since college days...

Friday evening's meal finished way past midnight and the various courses of dips and salads and kebab-type things were interspersed with drinks I just had to try. We didn't make it out of the apartment, let alone into the city centre. Ouzo, Tsipouro, Metaxà 5* and 7* and a B52 which Rachel thought she remembered how to make.

Richard must have gone home at some stage, because he wasn't there in the morning. Mind you, we haven't been able to find him by telephone today yet either. I woke up at seven, with a desperately full bladder, only to find that I had no idea where I was. I gradually worked out that I was on the sofa in the living room. A foot that was not my own was inches from my nose and did nothing to ease the feeling of nausea taking hold of me. Rachel was also on the sofa. Having extricated and then relieved myself, I actually contemplated trying to get back onto the couch. However, even in this drunken stupor, I wrote off this idea as being as far too complicated and potentially embarrassing. There were two guys on the T.V. loudly disagreeing about something, so I turned them off. I stumbled upstairs and crashed into my own bed where I slept through the entire day.

I surfaced for a couple of hours of resolute T.V. watching, for which I was silently joined by Rachel for a while before she half-heartedly raised a hand in defeat and disappeared to her room.

Today, on the contrary, I am refreshed and raring to go. I dragged a mildly-protesting Rachel from bed and onto the metro for Athens. Throughout our ride into the city we were besieged by the pathetic, blighted and poverty-stricken underbelly of Athenian society. A young mother with, I'm sorry to say, a far-from-beautiful child on her hip and a ten year old boy who deposited and then collected small pieces of paper with Greek script, which presumably explained his predicament. I felt very uneasy, but Rachel had the unseeing air of the other passengers on the train, resolutely ignoring the proffered hands. I gave a couple of coins to a girl playing a transistor radio, but apparently I was contributing to a child extortion ring which I shouldn't be encouraging, what with me being a teacher and all. I hadn't expected this type of thing. Nightmarish.

Greek sites of antiquity are free to the public on a Sunday! You can see the Acropolis from all over Athens, standing sentinel over the city. Against the brilliant blue backdrop of sky, the white marble columns are truly spectacular. Rachel seemed to find my enthusiastic ravings amusing, but said this was because it was good to hear someone impressed by this view which she had begun to take for granted. We climbed the hill to the Parthenon (which is the ruined temple). Apparently the hill itself, and all of the other ruined monuments and buildings, make up the actual the Acropolis. Without wanting to get all spooky and melodramatic, I must say that the feeling you get in that place is unreal. Sort of spooky and melodramatic. I've always enjoyed visiting historical bits in Britain, and particularly enjoyed the indefinable sense of history emanating from places such as Tintagel Castle and Glastonbury, but this is just another thing altogether.

The actual Parthenon was roped off from the ground-eroding feet of the legions of dedicated tourists, but what a building this must have been! This was where the Elgin Marbles once lived. Mental note to self to find out what they are. I feel a cultural Philistine out here. I stood for a while on the spot (or close to it, outside the site of the Temple of Athena Nike) where Aegeus supposedly killed himself when he saw his son's ship returning with a black sail. The son, Theseus, had killed the Minotaur but forgotten to raise a white sail as a symbol of his success. Okay, so I'm not quite a cultural Philistine; I do remember this story from Greek Mythology at school.

Rachel was infected by my enthusiasm, telling me again that it reminded her of how she felt when she first arrived. The view of the city from up there, clear because the traffic pollution was still light, was spectacular. We could see right across the cityscape to the sea and could just make out aeroplanes landing and taking off from the airport in the distance. As we walked down through the Ancient Agora (the bustling centre of the city since the 6th century BC, so the guide book tells me) there was a definite meeting of eyes and an uncomfortable silence. I put it down to the overawing sense of history around us: I don't want to get into uncomfortable silences and furtive glances.

We ate at a taverna called *'To Kouti'* nestled at the bottom of the hill. Apparently the green leafy salad that I like is called *horta* (pronounced with a hard 'ch' sound, which I can't do, and means grass). I'm also really into a fried cheese dish, the name of which I keep forgetting. Sounds something like Serengeti, but I'm sure that's not it.

On the train ride home, Rachel put her head on my shoulder and slept. It was really uncomfortable and so I put my arm around her and she definitely nuzzled in. I'm not convinced that she was sleeping the whole way, but she didn't move. Normally I would be dead chuffed about this, but I am trying to change things in my life, and I really don't want to go through another relationship crisis just yet. And I'm no good at the casual sex thing, especially with a house-mate. I'm beginning to like this girl a lot, more than I think I want to. I have hidden in my room since we got back and left her talking to the new arrivals. They probably think I'm really anti-social. Just now, they're right.

9

Monday 28th August

Rachel is nowhere to be seen this morning, which is possibly a good thing. Met the other girls properly last night and already don't think this is going to work. One has a cleaning mania, which is more than a little worrying, and the other is an airhead. Completely. As in 'nobody home'. Just one of the drawbacks of sorting out living arrangements through an accommodation agency in the UK.

I had two phone calls from England last night, and plenty of opportunity to gloat about my present circumstances. Joanne called this morning, something which she had promised not to do. She was trying hard not to sound tearful as she asked me how I was settling in. However, she soon started on about how we could have stayed together, how much she loved me and how we should see this as a challenge and not an obstacle and so on. She finally demanded to hear me say the words 'I don't love you.' I actually had to say, "I don't love you" and feel I am a shit. If I'd stayed, we'd be marching towards matrimony and premature parenthood. I know I've done the right thing. I think I know I've done the right thing. At the time when I did it, it felt like I was doing the right thing. Shit. She hung up, crying.

The airhead, who had actually been in the room during this conversation and had lacked the presence of mind to withdraw, chose this moment to ask if I liked her newly painted nails. Distant planets.

Goodbye, thank you and sorry
Turning points reached again
A new life springing
From the new
An old friend
Marginalised by the growth
of my inner self.

Unfair, but unfairer still
To feign affection
And to live a lie
To take hold
The proverbial bull
Kicking and snorting
To enter back

Into the realm
Of sorrow and guilt?

To emerge stronger
Strength drawn from
Being alone
I am
Finally
Me.
Thank you
For giving that
To me
I am sorry
That it took so much
Of you.

My other phone call was from friends who have now been married a couple of years. They triumphantly informed me that they were going to have a baby. I think I pissed them off a bit by asking them why, instead of offering hearty congratulations. I know I pissed them off a lot by asking why they thought they would be any good at it, since everyone I knew had been totally fucked up by their parents. It was a short call.

Tuesday 29th August

Sulked all day yesterday. Not sure at all if I've done the right thing. Am I missing her, or England, or sex? OK, definitely missing sex, but feel this could be good for my soul. Missing England? That's a nearly definite no.

Wednesday 30th August

I have to go to work tomorrow. Am depressed. My soul doesn't feel particularly good. Will go to find Rachel to drink gin with all afternoon - gin is always good for depression. Have read back over the last few entries and discovered to my surprise that I am missing many a personal pronoun. Odd.

Drank relatively little, as is evidenced by my still being able to write. It is 3.00am and I have four hours until I have to go to work. I spent hours talking to Rachel about her depression. She threw me a loop by saying she was seriously considering going back to Australia. Tasmania, to be exact. My stomach knotted. I have known this girl for little over a week; I am clear in my head that I don't want to get involved and yet... What am I doing? She was evidently surprised that I took off to bed and made no move beyond the delicate Platonic kiss goodnight. I have lain awake for a while, actually listening for her, willing her, in fact, to come to me. I must be mad.

Thursday 31st August

My first day of paid employment in Greece! Actually very similar to other days in school so far - tidying up and setting things out. Had a staff meeting. Took an instant dislike to one very prim-looking woman in her mid forties. She's the ex-pat personified. Very colonial. Discovered very shortly afterwards that I shall be team teaching with her. Oh joy! What did I do to deserve this?

Friday 29th September

So much for my resolve to write at least something in my diary every day. To catch up on a month's happenings...

Work's work, less good than it was promised to be, but bearable. The kids are great, if a little spoilt. Some of them probably get more pocket money than I earn, but that's life I guess. The parents are generally OK. Some, however, are uppity, pretentious, used to always getting their own way, interfering, condescending and not-very-nice people. One mother came in to tell me what exactly to teach her son. She'd like me to concentrate on reading, but she's not so bothered about maths just yet, and definitely no RE. I calmly explained, politely I thought, that we taught what we taught, that she had signed up for the school's existing curriculum and that, if she didn't like it, she could fuck off elsewhere. I didn't actually use the phrase 'fuck off', of course. Serious bollocking followed from Head, who advised me that we don't speak to 'these people' like that. I refused to apologise, however, and have made my first enemy here. I must resist the temptation to take it out on the kid as this would be puerile and unprofessional.

I haven't shagged Rachel, of which I am quite proud, in a perverse kind of way. However, it's quite possibly still out there. We talk a lot. She knows I want to steer clear of any kind of emotional entanglement, but thinks it's just a case of the 'right woman' coming along. She sounds very big sisterly from time to time. Inevitably, I've done the Joanne story. Somehow, in Rachel's eyes, I am sensitive and thoughtful and have the courage of my convictions. Joanne sees me differently. We have spoken

12

and I am indubitably a bastard. I did lead her on. I was unfair. I do hate myself. I will rot in Hell.

Rachel is unquestionably leaving Greece. I am going to miss her. Really miss her. She goes on the 15th of October and says she is not coming back. We both feel awkward during such conversations. Maybe we should just shag and get it over with. I accused her of running away and not facing up to her life. She rejoined with the same line and we agreed that this was an OK thing to do.

Have met interesting Danish woman a couple of times. Feel resolve is slipping. Perhaps I should experiment with casual sex. I seem to remember that it was more fun with someone else.

Tomorrow is my birthday. Have told everybody, including the kids at school. Big night out planned in *Kifissia*.

Actually, I don't really like the area where I live: a bit too posh for my tastes. A bit like Kensington. Kind of. Everyone's always dressed up, mobile phones and gold jewellery. There are designer clothes shops everywhere and dead expensive cafés and bars. It even has a Marks and Spencer's with a food hall - the height of ex-pat sophistication! I must go out drinking or eating (or both) five or six nights a week. (That's 'must' as in I think I do, not as in I have to.) Am definitely drinking too much here, though at least generally with company.

Saturday 30th September

Happy Birthday to me, Happy Birthday to me…

I am 28 years old, as of 3.01am this morning. We all stayed up to toast the precise hour of my birth, which was Rachel's idea. She kissed me, somewhat more passionately than I had reason to expect, and then said not to worry as it was my birthday and hence was allowed and didn't constitute the beginnings of a serious relationship. I think I'm glad. Am worried about getting drunk with her again though as I know just how weak willed I can be. Not sleeping with Rachel is becoming an obsession. She also bought me a *komboloi*, which is kind of like the Catholic Rosary, or worry beads, though without the religious aspect. Nice touch, I thought.

Received curt card from Joanne, saying 'Happy Birthday' and signed *from* Joanne. Mum also managed to get a card to me on time and some Belgian chocolates. I don't deserve such extravagance. Dad called from somewhere between flights in Europe, saying he'd send something from the Duty Free. It's the thought that counts.

Sunday 1st October

Oh shit. Have taken a step over the edge. Went to a range of bars last night and finished up at what is colloquially called 'The Hut'. Trudy showed up even though Rachel had said that she couldn't come. She had evidently changed her mind. She hadn't bothered to dress up - cut-off jeans, a short lace top and a brilliant smile. She insisted on buying me a birthday drink. At one point in the evening, I think I actually asked Rachel to make sure that she took me home and that I didn't disappear with Trudy. Rachel didn't appreciate such a blatant attempt to divest myself of any responsibility for my life and left shortly afterwards in something of a huff. In retrospect, I can't say I blame her.

Woke up this morning to Trudy sliding down the bed and a good morning kiss the likes of which I hadn't experienced before. In for a penny in for a pound...

When she suggested eating, I thought she meant to take a break from sex while we ate. She came back from the kitchen with a tray piled with all sorts of stuff. It was certainly an experience; I'll never look at pineapple rings in the same way again.

She's expecting me to ring tomorrow. She thinks I'm a nice bloke. I like her, and the sex is unbelievable... It's a no contest, I think. From a purely carnal point of view, this has to be explored further, although perhaps not for a couple of days. Still can't quite get over the pineapple rings...

Monday 2nd October

Have spent the day walking around as though I'd been on horseback for hours. Pretended I'd been cycling and was saddle sore. Must go and buy a bike. Didn't call Trudy and she didn't call me. It's now eight in the evening and I'm going to bed. Alone.

Tuesday 3rd October

Haven't called Trudy. Am feeling a bastard, again. Rachel's not really talking to me, beyond confirming that I'd stayed at Trudy's. "So much for celibacy then," she remarked, not entirely without a hint of sarcasm. As making the phone call is effectively starting a relationship, I am not going to call her. I don't have the strength for this.

Wednesday 4th October

Trudy came around last night and made me feel like a school boy who'd been caught shoplifting. "I'll save you the embarrassment of lying and saying you were going to call me," she began. Not a good start. Actually, she offered me a get out right there and then, saying it had been a great night and day and that we could just forget about it if that's what I wanted. Then she dashed apart any hopes I had of an escape with four simple words, "How about a blow-job?" What was I supposed to do, seriously? Very sleepless night. Very long day in work. Very nasty looks from Rachel. She's going in less than two weeks and I'm worried that we'll fall out over this. I'm going out with Richard tonight; I'll seek council.

Thursday 5th October

This has quite possibly been the longest and most difficult day of my life. The combination of sleepless nights with Trudy and last night with Richard created a living Hell: seriously knackered and hung-over in charge of fifty small children. The phrase, 'Never again' springs to mind, as it is wont to do in such situations.

I met Richard at eight last night. It seemed sensible to embark upon a couple of rounds of Amstel. I remember starting to talk about Rachel and Trudy and things. We seemed to get side-tracked into a discussion of the merits of Rachel's B52 cocktail and one thing led to another and we were traipsing from one bar to another in search of a comparable beverage. We had many more than was advisable. I managed to throw up on the way home. By some insane miracle of ignorance and will-power, I made my way into work the next morning. Richard, rather more intelligently, though perhaps somewhat unimaginatively, stayed in bed claiming flu.

Tonight I have succumbed to a variety of American TV shows, lots of incomprehensible adverts and no alcohol. Rachel is in a far better mood, and actually apologised for her exit the other evening. I was talking to her about Trudy, when Trudy phoned and asked if I'd like to go around. In deference to my ailing body I told her I'd call tomorrow. Rachel seemed pleased at this, though said nothing specific. I wasn't surprised to hear from Rachel that Trudy's nymphomaniac exploits did not begin with me, as much as my chauvinistic ego might have liked to believe it. I seem to recall Richard embarking on that theme last night. Rachel, the worse for most of a bottle of retsina, which I steadfastly refused to share with her, went on to describe in detail Trudy's predilection for an alternating orifice approach to the 'woman on top' position. I decided that the best response to this information was no response. Rachel professed to be appalled by this practice. No comment. Why do women share this kind of information? I retreated early from a potentially dangerous conversation.

Friday 6th October

Another week over, another holiday weekend begins. I am steering clear of alcohol for the entire weekend, no matter how cajoling others may be.

The big news is that the house situation is going to fold. With Rachel's leaving, the rent becomes too expensive for the three of us, not that I relish the prospect of staying here anyway. We're all looking for places to live. This is easier said than done, although I have help from a Greek-speaking friend who is scouring the newspaper this very minute.

There seem to be a few 'possibles' and we're going to try to arrange to see them tomorrow. Rachel's heard of a place nearby and is going to take me there later this evening. The few weeks of student-style living, while hectic and enjoyably social, have been enough. I find that I am looking forward to living on my own again, to settling down to something more staid.

Have just returned from looking at a beautiful little house in Kifissia. It has only two rooms, one of which is a kitchen. It's a bus ride to work, whereas currently I can just about walk. Unfortunately, it has no telephone either and people tell me that it's nigh on impossible to get a new line in under six months. I could buy a mobile, but I find them intrinsically naff. Plus expensive to use. Rachel really liked it – it is, as she says, cute - but as I pointed out, she wasn't going to live there with me, or even visit me there. This seemed to put things into perspective vis-à-vis her leaving and we walked home in silence. I don't think I want her to go. I called her Joanne this evening and she was decent enough to ignore it.

Have decided to call Trudy tonight to break things off. There's more to life than sex, however energetic it may be. I suspect that I will come to regret this decision...

Saturday 7th October

Called Trudy last night. She wasn't in. I must admit that I felt a certain relief. In the interests of not having to face her if she should come round, I took the cowardly but sensible option, I believe, and stayed out all night.

In the cold light of day, however, I have decided that I cannot live like this, avoiding my own house for fear that she'll turn up and make a scene. Am going to go round and get this over with.

Airhead and Cleaning Maniac have found someplace else to live and will be moving out sometime next weekend. That was quick!

Sunday 8th October

Yesterday was, erm, interesting. I'm still recovering, and this time not from alcohol poisoning. I went around to Trudy's flat unannounced. She was definitely unimpressed by my no-show of the day before. Having planned nothing at all to say, I blurted out the 'It's not you, it's me' speech and the 'I can't deal with being responsible for someone else's happiness' addendum, for good measure. Problem: in my mind this is virtually a non-relationship whilst to Trudy it is the beginnings of something deeply spiritual. And she's obviously seen 'Fatal Attraction'. This woman is not happy. Her "Don't think you can just walk away from me that easily!" was particularly scary. I left having been accused of lying to her, leading her on and taking advantage of her. One coffee cup (full) and one glass (empty) were hurled in my general direction. It appears that I am a bastard still.

I have been feeling a little isolated in recent weeks and this episode has done little to boost my self-confidence. I don't feel that I've done anything to be ashamed of, yet still feel at fault. Perhaps it's because Trudy's accusations, although groundless in relation to her, are identical to Joanne's. And Joanne had a point. I do feel that I was less than honest and fair and, therefore, a shit. However, I am looking out for me now. My happiness is important to me and, as far as possible, without intentionally setting out to hurt other people, I am going to do what seems to be best for me. And right now, 'best for me' translates as not becoming entangled with a mad Danish woman. I notice now that it was 'interesting' pre-coital and has become 'mad' post-coital. I wonder about the significance of this...

Trudy has phoned twice and Rachel has gamely lied for me on both occasions. She has also convinced me, for the time being, that I am not a shit. She quite justly demands what Trudy had expected and what gave her the right to such grandiose expectations. I feel better about myself, but realise that more and more often this feeling is dependent upon Rachel. I begin to worry about her leaving, not only because I'll miss her, but also because I think I need her around. This was why I didn't want to get close to anyone. I repeat to myself over and over, "I am responsible for my own happiness. I am the only person who can make me happy."

This is not particularly convincing, probably as I don't believe it. I seem to have managed to by-pass the sex part of this relationship and still feel all the shit dependency and insecurity part. *'Surely shome mishtake?'*, as "Private Eye" would put it.

Monday 9th October

Spent half an hour this morning trying to get one kid to recognise the first letter of his name. We decorated it, drew it in sand, painted it with water on the concrete outside and even made it with play dough. He copied it laboriously with crayon and pencil and chalk. I was convinced he'd got it. He encouragingly piped up with 'a' each time I showed him the letter on a flash card. Then, just before playtime, I thought I'd check one last time. "Four," he tells me happily. I think I must be in the wrong job. The thing about this job is that you're not allowed to beat the children.

No indication of anybody at home. No scarily threatening phone calls. Has to be a good sign.

Tuesday 10th October

It is about ten in the evening. I am gob-smacked. Trudy made an appearance shortly after I got home. Fearing the worst, I led her up to my room to keep the mad screaming and throwing of objects from the others, who were fortunately not back yet. She was impressively apologetic about the scene of our breaking up. Breaking up? Since when did two nights of shagging constitute a steady relationship? I thought it prudent, however, not to throw in this little query and just listen. As I did, she unfurled a story of disaster after disaster in her romantic escapades. We talked for a long time about expectations and responsibilities. I told her I had entered into our liaison (well, what do you call it?) with no expectations at all. She had entered into it, as with all her previous associations (her word, not mine: a Danish/English translation thing, I'm guessing) expecting Prince Charming to declare undying love and propose marriage. Oddly enough, he didn't tend to do that so often. I told her she tried too hard, which is probably what all the attentive and athletic sex was about. She said she always tried to make the other person need her physically and so always took control of sex and tried to overwhelm her partner. I told her that the overwhelm part was working OK. After a while she asked me if I wanted to make love to her, no strings attached, just for her, because I liked her as a person. She said she promised not to be mad again and pester me if I didn't want a girlfriend.

I am only human, and not a particularly moral specimen at that. She left later saying she hoped we could still be friends. I wonder if that arrangement has ever worked anywhere in the history of this little planet.

Wednesday 11th October

I feel I ought to be pleased with myself for last night. I'm not. I feel as though I have once again trampled all over someone's feelings. Plan to spend rest of the evening feeling sorry for myself.

Acts of loneliness
Straw-grasping
Futile and hurtful
Searching for viability
Craving love
But striking out
Acts of hatred
Aggression by another name
No answer here
Innocents used
Innocence abused
A mockery
A weakness of character
Intensely vulnerable
Intensely alone
Waiting on a miracle
Hoping for salvation
Dreaming of life
What am I doing?

Thursday 12th October

More of the same at work. It becomes clear that it will not be a source of energy for me. It has also become blindingly clear that the only source of energy I have found is Rachel, and she is leaving. I promised myself not to fall into the trap of relying upon someone else for my sense of well-being, and yet here I am again. Fuck.

I have started guitar lessons, in the hope that this will inspire me to great things. Fully intend to practise each day and become good at something. Will start practising tomorrow.

On the subject of lessons, I have also committed myself to starting Greek lessons, the first of which I had yesterday after school. I can now make out most of the alphabet and make an approximation of the sounds of words. Makes me realise what I've been putting kids through for the last few years. Easy it isn't.

I saw a great flat today. A colleague from work took me there this afternoon and I have agreed, possibly a little impulsively, to take it. It has an enormous lounge with wooden parquet flooring. It works out at about 200 quid a month, which I think I can cope with. It's further away from school, so I definitely do need to go and buy a bike. Richard says he'll take me to a cheap place in the centre of Athens this weekend.

Friday 13th October

Friday the thirteenth. Spooky! Another mind-numbingly dull day at work ('Yes, that's a lovely picture of a man. Oh, yes, I mean of your mum. Why are her arms growing out of the side of her face?' Anatomy is not your average four year old's strong suit.)

Caught the metro down to *Monastiraki* with Richard and bought a very cool-looking yellow mountain bike. Stopped off in Kifissia for a couple of beers before riding (fortunately downhill) back to the flat. We have decided that we are going to get fit together. This essentially beer-drinking relationship is going to evolve into a cycling-round-*Kefalari*-and-environs relationship. We'll see... Actually, there is more to Richard than meets the eye: he's a genuinely nice guy. He's actually responsible for my keeping at least one foot firmly on the ground in this fairy tale world I find myself living in.

It's now eight o'clock. I'm supposed to be getting ready to go out to a taverna with Rachael and a pile of friends. It's her leaving do. Her flight is on Sunday morning at six thirty, so she'll be leaving in a taxi at about 4am Saturday night/Sunday morning. This does not seem possible. I haven't really seen her this week, except in passing. Is she deliberately avoiding me, or am I sub-consciously avoiding her? She's not in again right now, so I'm guessing she'll go straight to the taverna. I feel an oppressive sense of gloom and despondency settling over me. I recognise this feeling of depression and had somewhat optimistically thought I'd left it behind in England. Quite clearly not. I feel that with Rachel gone, my life will have taken two steps backwards. Fuck. Again.

Haven't picked up the guitar or done my Greek homework.

So much for Friday 13th. Not at all spooky, as it turns out.

Saturday 14th October

Last night was a hugely drunken and debauched affair. It is now 4pm and I'm just about *compos mentis* enough to put pen, albeit shakily, to paper. Trudy was there, playing some sort of 'openly-flirtatious-make-you-jealous' type game with a guy who teaches Maths (or 'Math', as he would insist upon saying) at another school nearby. She kept looking over for a reaction: I imagine she'll have been disappointed.

Richard and I toasted, several times, our new found fitness regime. He, at least, did cycle to the taverna.

The waiter kept producing large carafes of a murky-looking white wine which had a kick like the proverbial mule. Said carafes kept disappearing as they were liberally poured out and various toasts drunk to an increasingly tearful Rachel. Before the end of the evening she had been sick in the garden of the taverna within earshot of the neighbouring table, much to their disgust and had told Vangelis, the waiter, that she loved him. (While I remember, that fried cheese is called *saganaki*. I wrote it down so that I could actually order it on my own sometime.)

I took Rachel home with the help of Siobhan (the cleaning maniac) and her airhead friend, who doesn't deserve a name. Both were somewhat disapproving of our drunken states and very much looking forward to their impending move to a more civilised apartment. In my drunken state, my resolve not to sleep with Rachel would have cracked with only the slightest encouragement. Fortunately, perhaps, she passed out immediately upon being deposited on her bed. I did the same shortly afterwards.

Was woken this morning by the sounds some very loud Greek guys carting boxes downstairs. I think the girls may have moved out already. It has gone quiet, at least. Am going to see if I can monopolize Rachel's remaining hours here.

Still haven't picked up the guitar or learnt the Greek verb ειμαι, "to be", which is apparently a fairly crucial one to get to grips with.

Monday 16th October

I am not in work today. I had thought that before very long I'd miss a day through impending alcoholism, but today's absence has another cause. I phoned in sick, claiming to have fallen foul of a nose and throat bug which has been doing the rounds.

I found Rachel somewhat the worse for wear when I got up on Saturday afternoon. She was staring at the TV, watching 'The Nanny', a less-than cerebral American sitcom. She chose this moment to tell me that she didn't know what she was doing with her life, and maybe leaving Greece was the wrong thing to do, and what if and what if...

Predictably enough, this revelation ended in tears. In an attempt to re-direct her attentions elsewhere, I suggested that it might be an idea to start packing. She had made no incursions into this project what-so-ever. She did, however, have a valid airline ticket - I'd asked to see that earlier, when I didn't believe that she was going.

We stormed through the clothes packing in no time at all and emptied the desk and drawers into boxes to take upstairs to sort through. (Rachel's room is a glorified cellar downstairs, benefiting hardly at all from natural light.) This done, there was only the matter of a few ornament-type things, life-affirming bric-a-brac, to pack. She was in something of a reckless mood, and we trashed quite a lot of stuff which probably she will regret having trashed. We took her metallic rubbish bin outside to the balcony, lit a fire in it and fed the flames a diet of old letters and postcards. She even burnt some perfectly decent clothes which she said she'd probably never wear again. In this manner, I inherited a few pictures, an electric fire (though God knows what anyone would want with an electric fire in this climate), assorted books, a sandwich toaster and a duvet which smells distractingly of Rachel.

We took everything upstairs and left an empty room behind us. It was clear that she still had too much stuff to carry on a plane and we sorted out a box which I would look after for her. It was quite clear, though, that she wouldn't be coming back. We'd opened a bottle of gin by this stage, the bottle being Rachel's and my argument being that she couldn't take it with her and it wasn't fair to leave it here for me to drink in a state of depressed loneliness. However, after a glass or two, neither of us felt much like drinking and for a while we just fell to talking. She said that it was funny, because if she hadn't been leaving we'd have probably slept together by now and I'd be avoiding her as I was avoiding Trudy, instead of sitting here holding her hand. This surprised me, as I hadn't realised I was holding her hand. I loosened my grip and she said, 'Don't,' and before I knew it we were kissing and Rachel was crying and then we were kissing again.

Unbelievably though, we stopped there and held one another for what seemed like ages before I felt myself nodding off and found that Rachel had also fallen asleep. I woke her, somewhat ridiculously, to ask her if she wanted to sleep. It wasn't until then, of course, that we realised we'd packed her entire room away. I offered her my bed and went up with her and set the alarm clock for three. That way she would have four hours sleep before her taxi arrived. When I looked up from the clock, Rachel was standing at the foot of the bed in just her cut-off jeans, her blouse and bra lying on the floor. She looked me in the eye as she unbuttoned her shorts and stepped out of her underwear. "I hope you're planning on coming to bed with me," she said. She didn't make any kind of move after that. It was weird, I just looked at her, and she just stood there. It must have been minutes before I touched her, walking around her and feeling every part of her body. She had the smoothest skin I'd ever felt. Every touch was electric. It was a unique and spiritual experience.

The alarm woke me from a very deep sleep. Rachel wouldn't hear of my getting up. She put all of her things by the front door and then came back up to my room. With the French window open, and lying the wrong way round on the bed, we could see the road and would hear the taxi arrive. And much more frantically, we made love again.

I offered to ride to the airport with her, but it must have sounded very lame, because she didn't take it as a serious offer at all. Just then I would have gone anywhere with her. As the taxi sounded its horn she was pulling on her clothes, the long jeans and a sweatshirt she'd put aside for the flight. She kissed me goodbye and said, "Dream of me," as she left.

I heard the taxi doors close. All I could do was cry.

I spent most of Sunday sleeping. When I woke I had a manic tidy up. The girls came back to collect a few kitchen things and to say goodbye to Rachel. Airhead had thought she was leaving today. When they left, the emptiness of the flat was oppressive, echoing an emptiness inside me. I don't like this place any more - already too many memories. Sunday evening was tortuously long; I was just waiting for sleep. I couldn't stand the feeling of being alone. When I eventually went up to bed, helped by some of the remaining gin, I realised for the first time that I had not left my demons behind me in England, but had brought them all along for the ride. Bastards.

Today I am spending alone with my thoughts.

> *An ode to a sad Talisman*
> *Forgotten?*
> *Never known*
> *Made up,*
> *Imagined,*
> *Dreamt of.*
> *In my mind's eye*
> *Perfection lies*
> *Deception lies*
> *At the end of the world*
> *Begins the new*
> *The 'you'*
> *Here I am*
> *I'm almost all I can be*
> *-Take me…*

Tuesday 17th October

The poet within me has awoken through depression! Perhaps he was better off sleeping. I have taken today off work as well, on the premise that a two day bug has a ring of authenticity about it. Have re-read Richard Bach's "Illusions" and am feeling all spiritual again. Am starting "A Bridge Across Forever".

11pm: It's the first time since "War and Peace" that I have sat down and read a book from cover to cover without stopping (and that didn't really count as it was for a substantial bet and I did sleep for two nights in between reading).

I can't get my head around how I feel. I am beginning to feel unwell, which is perhaps the result of too much introspection. It's just occurred to me that I haven't eaten since yesterday morning, which is probably a more likely cause. I think I'll skip tomorrow too.

Wednesday 18th October

It's ten in the morning. I have just received a phone call from Abigail, a nurse and friend of the French teacher at school. She said she'd heard I was ill, asked how I was and did I want anything from the Pharmacy (by which I assume she meant chemist). She's picking up some Aspirin and lemons and honey and says she'll drop round after lunch. I find myself wondering why she should call. I've only spoken to her a couple of times when we'd met in town and she always seemed very aloof. I now have to tidy up a little. Am definitely feeling very unwell; I think I have a genuine temperature.

I do indeed have a temperature and will probably miss the rest of the week. Am now beginning to feel guilty about this; but not very, because no bastard I work with has even called to see how I am. I could be dying here for all they know.

Abigail came round and stayed for an hour or so. Apparently, she's Abby to her friends, but Abby sounds like a building society to me, so I stuck to her full name, which she said she liked and found "sweet of me". Hmm. She brought medicines and made hot drinks but was not fooled by my dying swan act. She noticed the Bach books and we talked about them for a while - we seemed to be very much on the same wavelength. My first literary conversation since coming out here. Come to think of it, my first real conversation about life, the Universe and everything. I'm intrigued.

At the same time I see a barely discernable sadness in her eyes. She avoids direct questions about herself, which is always a warning sign to stay away. No complicated entanglements. She seemed to take pity on me for my rattling around on my own in such a huge flat and for the sudden departure of flatmates. I told her I'd found a place and was moving in at the end of the month. When she asked me how I was going to move my stuff, I realised that this problem had not occurred to me. I have inherited much: not only things from Rachel, but also odds and ends of furniture left in the house, including a three piece suite, a cooker and a fridge. Abigail said she might be able to find a pick-up truck and give me a hand if I tell her when. I promised to give her a call. She stresses that this is a 'maybe' in such a way as I already suspect she wishes she hadn't offered. As she left, for some reason I asked her if she'd like to pop by again anytime she might be passing as I'd enjoyed talking to her. I'm thinking, "Where did that come from?" She said she might.

I'm doped up with Paracetemol. I've brought a sleeping bag downstairs and plan to spend the night with crap Greek telly

Friday 20th October

I have actually been more ill than I'd thought. Yesterday morning, another colleague from work came around and, upon seeing me wrapped up on the sofa, immediately took me to see a doctor. He took a cursory look at my throat and glands before writing out a prescription for antibiotics. I was then deposited back on the sofa at home, and told that Richard would pop in on the way home.

Richard showed up, characteristically offering whiskey as the ultimate cure-all. Neither of us could remember if you weren't supposed to drink with antibiotics because the alcohol stopped them from working or because it got you drunk quicker. We plumped for the latter, in which case a couple of measures of Jameson's could hardly do me much harm. We had a poetry writing session, always a good idea if you're feeling maudlin and generally sorry for yourself. I was quite impressed with my effort, which I found this morning on a paper napkin:

> *Whiskey talks*
> *Politicians pontificate and amuse*
> *Friends sympathise and accuse*
> *Enemies lie and abuse*
> *But whiskey,*
> *Whiskey just talks.*

Richard also brought a video to wile away a couple of hours, but I fell asleep shortly after it started and when I woke up it had finished. Another groggy early night. I don't think the whiskey helped.

Today, Abigail came around after her early morning shift, with an enormous Doberman in tow. Or, I should say, an enormous Doberman came around, with Abigail in tow. "You're not scared of dogs, are you?" she asked, as it careered around the lounge, bounding over the furniture and smashing mugs and discarded plates. The dog absolutely refused to settle, so we took it out for a walk. This seemed strangely familiar. What is it about this woman which makes me feel so peaceful? She said she might be round on Friday evening with the truck. I asked where she managed to find a pick-up truck, and she dismissed the question rather vaguely.

Again warning bells ring loudly. Knowing better, of course, I ignore them. Again.

Saturday 21st October

> *A moody eye cast downward*
> *Over the madding crowd,*
> *A milling headless multitude*
> *Pre-programmed by the Fool.*
> *Its listless limbs thrash,*
> *Without aim, reason or intent,*
> *At the good-intentioned advice-givers*
> *Plaguing its solitude and self-pity.*
> *Thought trips over thought*
> *In that Jester's mind*
> *As ultimately it sighs defeat*
> *And, apathy belying hope, it seeks another toy.*

Not a good day. I need to get out and be busy. A mild depression falls upon me again, thoughts of Rachel. I have to do something!

> *And now, Life itself looks questioningly at me,*
> *Mocking my indecision,*
> *Relishing my fears,*
> *Feeding, with insincerity,*
> *Upon my tears.*

Sunday 22nd October

It's official: the honeymoon period of my move to Greece is over. Everything seems heavy and slow and too much effort. I began packing for the move today, far too early, but just to have something to do. I feel intensely sad about myself and where I am - so much for life in Paradise.

> *Not a thought in my head is my own*
> *Each feeling is borrowed*
> *Each nuance a plagiarism*
> *And each sincerity a fake*

Look into my eyes.
You will see
A façade I want you to see
Not me.
I am unavailable for comment,
A charlatan with faded dreams,
And subsiding means,
Heaven-sent.

Plainly my mood is not a good one. I have to stop thinking about Rachel's leaving as though it were a personal insult to me. It's a classic 'glass half empty/glass half full' scenario. I could look on what has happened as a beautiful memory to cherish, and recognise how lucky I have been. As she said, if she hadn't been leaving perhaps everything would have gone sour by now anyway. And in any case, I was the one who didn't want to get at all involved, so I should quite definitely be happy. I am the same free spirit who arrived in Greece determined to be positive and to look out for myself. So, get a grip!

I think I need to get very drunk. However, not a good idea as I have to work tomorrow and convince people that I actually know what I'm doing and give a damn.

Monday 23rd October

A dose of reality was just what I needed. I am resolving to be more positive about work. Whilst I definitely do not enjoy this environment on the whole, it was good to see people again and to be busy enough to stop thinking for a while. And I have to keep reminding myself that the kids are lovely: rant about them from time to time as I do in the privacy of my diary, they are endearing and cute and rewarding as only four and five year olds can be.

Richard is cooking pizza tonight and there's some English football on the box. It's nothing but culture out here!

The pizza was good, the football less so, and the company and the beer made a welcome change from recent days. Going to sleep now, a bit drunk and a lot happier.

Tuesday 24th October

I managed to go in with odd socks today. One patterned red and the other plain green, not even close. One of my more observant little cherubs asked me why my socks were 'oddly'. I told them I had another pair at home just like this one, but such sarcasm was clearly way over their heads... Oh well.

I actually fell asleep during the staff meeting. Was kicked awake by Richard.

Wednesday 25th October

In a perverse kind of way, I am enjoying teaching. Actually, that's not fair; I quite often enjoy teaching; it's the mindless bureaucracy, not to mention the anally retentive bureaucrats, that I generally can't deal with. For now, however, I seem to be able to float above all the bickering and petty internal politics (with a very small and insignificant 'p'). I feel somehow unconnected to all of this. It's a feeling I remember from childhood: being a little displaced, almost a spectator and hence without the responsibility of real life. I don't feel superior exactly (though I'll admit in these pages that it does sound that way) but just detached and peaceful amidst the building chaos. Just now, it suits me fine!

In this mood, I bump into Abigail as I leave school. I hadn't seen her at all this week. I asked if she'd been OK. Apparently so, but she says she just arrives for her lessons (she teaches some after-school French groups a couple of times a week) and then disappears as quickly as possible because she can't stand all the pettiness of the place. Uncanny.

Before I know what I'm doing, I have invited her around to eat tonight. This is a stupid thing to have done for three reasons:

1. There is no food whatsoever in the house as I am moving out on Friday and am living off a limited range of toasted sandwiches.

2. I have packed everything vaguely useful in the way of kitchen equipment with the nebulous notion that I may use them in my new place.

3. I can't cook.

By way of accepting, she asks if it's okay to bring the dog.

That was lunchtime. It is now five, and I have three hours to go shopping, cook something edible and try to make both the flat and myself a little presentable.

Thursday 26th October

Dinner was a success last night! I opted for spaghetti and a salsa sauce which I figured even I couldn't screw up. I even added garlic, onions and oregano and grated cheese to go on top: it felt like proper cooking. I chose a French wine, a Bourgogne, sub-consciously trying to impress. We talked about writing, books we'd read, classical music (about which I know less than nothing) and living as a foreigner in Greece. I can really talk to this woman. She seems to be able to reach inside of me and draw out the good parts, the parts I like, and make me feel that I am someone. She still emanates a tangible sadness, which I feel is something far beyond anything I've encountered before. I find myself intrigued.

For the first time in a long time, possibly years, I put a half full bottle of wine back in the fridge with one of those plastic sealing cork stopper things. I went to bed happy and sober.

Predictably enough, not much guitar practice or Greek revision took place. I must do something about the latter, as lessons are somewhat embarrassing, not to say pointless, when I show up having forgotten what I supposedly learnt last time.

I have arranged with my Greek teacher to move my stuff in his very old Datsun tomorrow evening at six. Abigail may or may not show. She is clearly a woman who likes to keep her options open. Tonight I have to pack everything into the boxes I have purloined from behind the supermarket across the road.

Friday 27th October

School finished today! Waving goodbye to the kids actually brought an emotional sting to my eyes – what's that about? I must be mellowing in my old age.

I now have a week's holiday in which to settle into my new place. I find I am perked up considerably by the prospect of living on my own. Somewhat prematurely, I am having a house-warming on Saturday night. I thought I'd wait for a week, but Richard says that this way, I'll get loads of house-warming-type presents and may find I don't need to buy quite so much stuff. It wouldn't have occurred to me, but it does make sense. He's been there, done it.

I'm all set and waiting for Spiros. I have just borrowed the trolley thing from school to shift the fridge and the cooker.

Saturday 28th October

I'm in! I'm sitting in my lounge, drinking coffee made in my kitchen, watching my telly and feeling generally chuffed with myself.

Spiros and I had just filled his car with the first load, when Abigail pulled up in the half-promised pick-up. I was genuinely surprised to see her, and inexplicably happy (well, not inexplicably, but there are things going on here I'm not yet ready to admit to myself). We managed to do the whole move in just two trips, which was a huge relief. The landlady came out as we were loading the truck and said that I should take everything from the flat, as it had all belonged to previous tenants and she would throw away anything left behind. So, I got a dining table and chairs, a set of three coffee tables, a whole load of plates and cups and the like, a standard lamp and assorted potted plants. Hence my new place looks almost lived in already.

It took us until about 10.30 p.m. to get everything in, and then Spiros had to get back home. I must go and get him some wine or something, to say 'thank you'. As we hadn't eaten, I offered to take Abigail out to a restaurant nearby. She took some persuading. She was cold and beginning to suffer from the flu bug I'd had before. Walking into a restaurant with her, sharing a meal and climbing into her car afterwards all felt so familiar and right, it was almost as if I had done these things before.

It's strange: I have always felt before that I adapt myself to other people; I try to anticipate their interests; I think about what they might want to hear. It's crazy, I know, but it's a sub-conscious thing I've always done - right down to choosing the music I put on when someone is around. It's as though I've always been afraid to display myself, for fear of judgement. It is the same with Abigail; I do try to find her interests. I find myself remembering French from twelve years ago in school and I tell her how keen I am to learn again. But something is different. I feel I don't need to play games, to pretend to be something I'm not. I don't feel there's anything I can't talk about with her, and yet I've only known her a few days.

Then again, I felt very close to Rachel after a very short time. Perhaps, contrary to my assertions, I'm simply returning to form.

31

No. Not this time. I am definitely going to be on my own for some time. I don't need another person's approval to believe in myself, or another person's love to feel I deserve to be loved. Well, actually I do, but in an ideal world I shouldn't. I'm aiming for the ideal here.

We got back to my place just after midnight, and she politely refused the offer of a drink, preferring to drop me off outside. I was glad, when I got in, to be here on my own. I ran out again to give her the Paracetamol she'd bought me (amazingly enough I found them straight away in one of the kitchen boxes). She is definitely not well and I said I felt responsible, as she'd probably caught it from me. She said so I should, and that she probably had, which threw me entirely off balance, not being the prescribed British polite dismissal of such a silly notion. She also turned down my invitation to the house-warming tonight, and gave no reason, which also struck me as odd: just to say, "No, thanks," was discordant and ever-so slightly unsettling.

I was quite proud of myself that I didn't go on to ask what she was doing for the holidays or ask for her number or suggest she pop around another time. So who's not playing games? I wanted to do all these things, but didn't want to sound too keen. Now, I'm glad that I didn't. I must also admit, however, that I went through all my staff list information from school and being unable to find her phone number, I persuaded Veronica, the French teacher, to give it to me. This doesn't mean I'm going to use it, of course. It just feels good to have.

So now, having become quickly bored by the endless soaps and crime series on TV, I'm sitting outside in the brilliant sunshine. I have even been strumming a few chords on my guitar. My ground floor apartment has a large marbled area outside with plastic garden furniture. Just earlier, the neighbours from upstairs came down and left me a plate of biscuits and some very sweet honeyed cakes. I managed to make it understood that I was learning Greek and they seemed pleased by this. I've made myself a frappé. When I've finished this I'm going to go for a wonder and explore my new neighbourhood.

Sunday 29th October

I'm truly glad that I now have a week off work, because this hang-over is going to hang on for a few days. And to think it all started with a small sip of Tsiporou at about eight o'clock yesterday evening when Richard arrived with some others from school in tow. Everybody seemed to have brought a bottle of spirits as well as a carrier bag full of Amstel. I even did the guided tour a few times. My oddest present, but potentially most useful, was a toilet seat. Spent half an hour fixing said item to its proper place - a job which no doubt should have taken two minutes.

Trudy showed up with a few girls I'd never seen before, the music was blaring (DJ Richard at the controls – some obscure British band that nobody else had heard of) and those so-inclined were dancing. Various people had brought food as well, which was an unexpected bonus. I'd gone to the trouble of opening some bags of crisps and looking out the pizza delivery phone number.

My memory is hazy after this point. I remember dragging Maria, a friend of Trudy's, into the bathroom and enforcing a cold shower. This was, though, after considerable provocation. There ensued a ritual soaking of everybody still present - it must have been about two in the morning. The old lady from upstairs had been down to ask us to be a little quieter; a good start on neighbour relations. At some point, we realised we were all very cold and had no dry clothes. In two cars (no, I have no idea) we got to Richard's house where we all raided his wardrobes and drawers for anything to wear. I think the dressing in dry clothes was the stage at which Richard and Renata disappeared from the scene and left the rest of us to it. Renata was a friend of Rachel's; I do vaguely remember Richard and I had talked a bit about her on the night of the B52 fiasco. At some stage I decided to walk a little for the fresh air and actually managed to walk home. Some feat, I don't think I could have found my way sober.

In any event, I don't remember getting home but I do recall waking up this morning to a concerned call from Trudy asking what had happened to me. This story, so far, has taken me all day to put together.

Trudy and Maria came around a little while ago and helped me to dry the place and to hang out all the clothes and cushions. We really had managed to make quite a mess - I'm glad I hadn't unpacked everything. They want to go to an island for a couple of days, since the weather seems to be holding. (Holding? Apparently, it's going to get cold and wet in the winter!) They talked me into going with them, although I am having doubts now about the wisdom of going anywhere with Trudy, however innocent the invitation appears. But no, sod it. I want to go, so why shouldn't I? I'm not leading her on by accepting an invitation to go to an island, with a friend of hers.

I have phoned and we are going to Aegina tomorrow morning. They'll pick me up in a taxi at ten and there's a boat from Piraeus at 11.30am. I'm really looking forward to this! My first visit to an island! I've found my guide book and read a little about it - it's only an hour away. Why haven't I done this before, instead of drowning my weekends in Amstel?

Monday 30th October

Spent yesterday evening watching "The Great Escape", for what must have been about the twentieth time. During one of the interminable advert breaks, I found myself watching the phone, as though expecting a call, and wondering what Abigail was up to. The sudden ringing then almost gave me a coronary. It was Rachel. She'd got my new number from Richard and, since I hadn't called, she thought she'd see how I'd settled in.

She'd actually phoned to say that she'd like to stay in touch by letter every now and then but didn't want to expect phone calls and then worry about why I hadn't called. It was nice.

I agreed that I would only call her on odd occasions and not make it a regular thing that she would come to expect; it's hardly as though we can conduct a love affair from so far away! I told her that I thought, in a way, we were lucky, because we'd always remember how great it was, and we never had the time to start to feel disillusioned. It was actually a rather dispiriting call as, in the end, both of us kind of ran out of things to say. I hung up feeling surprisingly little. Dare I admit that part of me was even glad that she'd gone? Maybe I am a bastard. Plain and simple.

Anyway, bastard or not, I'm off to Aegina for a few days of sunshine and beaches and relaxation...

Thursday 2nd November

My first visit to an island was almost an unmitigated disaster. Trudy's friend did a no-show. In retrospect this is not surprising. How naïve am I? Anyway, since I was all packed and genuinely looking forward to the trip, I figured I'd go anyway. We were both consenting adults and whatever happened was going to be on my terms. The ferry ride was great: really choppy and lots of rolling from side to side. I like that kind of thing, but judging from Trudy's very green pallor, she was not such a fan. I refused to start out assuming responsibility for her sea-sickness and playing the caring, concerned partner; I left her to it. I was angry with her for setting me up anyway, so I guess I thought she deserved it. Not a good start.

We arrived in Aegina Town in glorious sunshine. We hired a moped from one of the two places still open. It appeared that much of the touristy stuff on the island had already closed for the season. It also turned out that my Greek was almost on a par with Trudy's. I had somehow assumed she was pretty much fluent. Luckily, the moped guy was a Greek-American and spoke excellent English. Luckily also, he didn't seem at all interested in seeing if I knew how to ride a moped and just disappeared inside, leaving us to it. I was surprised that he didn't come straight back out and take the keys off me, in view of the awful noises I was making with his bike. I guess they're used to holiday makers hiring bikes and not having a clue how to ride them.

We made our way to Perdika, where we planned to stay. We had arrived mid-afternoon and it seemed that the village was sleeping. We eventually found a place advertising *domatia* or rooms. The woman seemed surprised to find people looking for somewhere to stay - not a good sign. Anyway, the room was okay: twin-bedded, which I thought was fortunate. The old woman seemed intent on showing us the blankets in the wardrobes and telling us there were more in the open room next door. There were five rooms in the apartment and we were the only occupants. We found a tiny little shop, grandiosely declaring itself to be a supermarket, and bought feta cheese, bread and some salad stuff. Back at the room we unpacked and ate on the balcony, slowly drinking wine and watching the sun descend and then finally disappear.

We crashed out early, both of us avoiding the issue and taking to separate beds.

I woke up early, feeling cold and wondering what the strange drumming sound was outside. When I opened the shutters, we were greeted by a torrential downpour and a howling gale. I got back into bed without a word and we watched the weather. I wasn't at all surprised when Trudy came back from the bathroom and slid into my bed. After all, what else was there to do?

We tried sightseeing, but travelling on the bike was ridiculously cold, and neither of us had waterproof anythings. We made it to Agia Marina on the bus one day and sat around in various cafés, drinking coffee we didn't really want, just to keep warm. In Perdika, we found one open taverna which had a fire inside – Manos, the South African-Greek owner, it managed to come up with something without meat for me. Trudy had some kind of fish, which she says was excellent. The next evening, after wandering around the village in the rain for half an hour, we ended up back in the same taverna. He had prepared a wonderful vegetarian paella and a range of traditional Greek side dishes. I was amazed, but he explained that he knew we'd be back because there was nowhere else open in the village. He asked us what we'd like the next day.

I suppose not surprisingly we ended up in bed very early each evening and stayed there until fairly late each morning. There was a single portable electric hotplate for cooking; we moved it to the foot of the beds and left it on all night in an attempt to keep warm. I couldn't believe how cold it could get!

On the Wednesday morning we took off for the port with the intention of heading back to Athens. The boats weren't running because of the extreme weather; we could try again tomorrow. That's when we took the bus to Agia Marina, principally because we were wet, cold and on a bike, and the bus looked warm and dry.

We managed to get a boat on Thursday morning and arrived in Piraeus to more of the same weather. On the boat, I explained to Trudy that I had no intention of seeing her on a regular basis when we got back. I didn't put it quite so bluntly. She said she thought I'd change my mind if she was persistent enough. I told her I was sure I wouldn't, and that she was only going to get hurt if she carried on like this. She then demanded to know why I'd come, and why I'd slept with her again. Deciding that this was one of those 'cruel-to-be-kind' moments, I told her that I found the sex interesting, but not her, particularly. I accept that this could have been phrased better. She didn't respond at all. We found a taxi and drove in silence to her flat. All the while, I was getting closer and closer to caving in and apologising, telling her that I didn't mean that exactly and that I did like her; I managed to say nothing, however. When we arrived, she collected her bag from the back of the cab. She had tears in her eyes as she leaned into the taxi and slapped me across the face.

"You're just like all the others. You're a bastard and you know it, I think!" With that she stormed off.

The taxi took me home. And yes, I do know it.

Friday 3rd November

Spent last night in melancholic retrospection. Again.

I suffer from dual responses when I try to work out how I feel about this situation. My head is clear on the matter: I was duped into going with her on my own. I didn't promise her anything, either verbally or by way of leading her on. She wanted to sleep with me, and her expectations thereafter were her problem. On the other hand, emotionally, I feel one hundred percent to blame. I slept with her again, knowing she was expecting more. I have thus acted like a complete shit.

However hard I try, I cannot seem to reach a consensus. No doubt I shall go on feeling guilty for a time, whilst knowing that this is not justified and so hate myself for not being rational. Great.

Saturday 4th November

Spent yesterday and today unpacking boxes in the kitchen and generally tidying up. Deliberately kept busy to avoid sitting down and writing more depressing poetry. I also wired up the cooker and am pleasantly surprised that it seems to be working. The fridge has a peculiar anomaly, however, in that whenever one opens the door, the inside light comes on and the fuses in the rest of the flat blow. Hence have removed the bulb from the fridge as this seemed to me to be the easiest option.

I cooked myself a chilli: I opened a variety of tins and mixed them together before heating them up with chilli powder. It's a start. I have no alcohol in the house and bought none when I went shopping. I may regret this later, but for now feel pleased with myself.

I've neither seen nor heard from anyone in two days and I must say I don't feel particularly depressed about this. Could it be that for the first time in twenty eight years, I am actually beginning to enjoy my own company? Well, enjoy is perhaps too strong a word: but not detest it, at least. I have spent some constructive time thinking about Trudy and have decided that I am not going to hate myself for somebody else's problem, which is essentially what this is. I have for too long been a slave to other people's feelings, or at least my perception of them. Bollocks to it! I am not responsible for anyone else's problems or for creating or maintaining anyone else's happiness. It's high time I spent more effort worrying about my own.

I feel a poem coming on:

> *Battling,*
> *Inwardly trying*
> *To promote the cause*
> *Of the optimist within himself*
> *Sensing the darkness*
> *The power*
> *Of the cynic*
> *Dragging him downwards*
> *He turns from his tawdry fears*
> *Looks, not to the future*
> *But to the 'now'*
> *And asks, "Am I happy?"*
> *He realises*
> *For the first time*
> *That he can honestly answer,*
> *"Yes, I am."*

Sunday 5th November

Last night was Bonfire Night at the school. Apparently I was supposed to go. I had completely forgotten about it. Apparently there will be repercussions tomorrow. Richard clearly enjoyed telling me this. I suspect this is bullshit. We're going out for a pizza this evening. I am not going to get drunk and work with a hangover again tomorrow. I'm not, I'm not, I'm not!

Monday 6th November

Managed just the one beer last night and feel very proud of myself. Richard thinks I'm ill.

No repercussions from my non-attendance at the bonfire. The kids all noticed, however, and have been asking me all day where I was.

Today was my first cycle ride into school. It takes me five minutes on the way down and twenty-five on the way back up. Who knows, maybe I'll even get fit this way? I have a problem though, in that it is now unquestionably winter. Nobody told me about this when I took the job.

Am not impressed. On the ride home I cannot wear all the clothes I need to wear to keep warm on the way down in the morning. I can see me making a collection of jackets and jumpers at school. I have also begged and borrowed said items from colleagues, as it didn't occur to me to bring them with me from England. They have been most generous. I had been under the impression that it would be a tropical paradise here. All year round. And me with a Geography degree and all. Just goes to show…

I have radiators in the flat, but no means of controlling them. This is apparently normal in Greece. The landlord, who lives on the top floor, puts them on when he feels like it, and I have to make the best of the heat I get. I can at least have hot water when I want it. So, I've discovered a use for Rachel's electric fire after all. I took the opportunity to send her a postcard informing her of this. Richard tells me that last year they had two days off school because of snow!

Friday 10th November

Only my second real lapse in diary entries since I started in August. I'm quite proud of myself.

A long week in work, with Parents' Evenings and loads of crap paperwork due in next week. When I have weeks like these, I have to consciously remind myself that I'm in this job for the holidays. (Teaching in England was good in that respect: five and a half weeks off during the summer. Here, it's going to be ten! And three at Christmas and two at Easter and a couple more thrown in for half terms. It does seem to make the hassle worthwhile.)

I saw Abigail in school and she's had a really bad week. She was laid up with flu. From what I could gather, without asking direct questions of course, she lives on her own. I felt guilty that I had been away: she, after all, came to see me when I was ill and when she hardly even knew me. Here I am, feeling some kind of empathic link with her, and I bugger off for the week when she's ill. There goes my dual response dilemma again: my head knows I ought to feel no guilt at all. For what, after all? I instinctively feel at fault all the same.

I told her about my trip to Aegina, maybe as some kind of sub-conscious way of telling her that I wasn't off having a great time while she was ill. Why do I feel I owe her any kind of explanation? She asked if no-one had told me the islands were like that in October. Cheers. Actually, I told her *all* about Aegina, the Trudy factor and all, determined to be up front and honest with her about absolutely everything. Abigail simply looked at me, lips pursed, and didn't comment.

Feeling empowered by my new sense of self, I called her this evening to ask if she fancied going to a Lebanese restaurant which someone in work had told me about. It's amazing what a flat refusal can do to destroy a guy's new found self-assurance. Am not going to sulk all evening though.

Saturday 11th November

Pretty much sulked all evening, though thinly disguised as watching TV.

Was therefore extremely surprised to hear a knock on the door this morning, at eleven, and to see her standing there. Did I fancy going with her to walk the dog?

Now that I am back, again sitting outside in the sunshine, I can hardly believe what I'm feeling. If I close my eyes, I can be there again, not just as a memory, but actually there…

The dog ran on ahead, stopping frequently to look back at us, head cocked questioningly, before he ran on again, tongue flapping and saucer-feet padding the ground playfully, in search of a new distraction. We weren't talking - not about anything important at least. We were just being. It was one of those almost frosty November days: our breath rose visibly and lost itself amongst the dappled confusion of bright sunlight and leaf shadow. I looked across at her from time to time, taking in her profile, her smile… Once, just once, she caught my look and held it momentarily. In that instant I lived a lifetime. In that look there was a world of knowing. She was saying, "Yes, I understand you." I felt safe: the playing was over and this could be why I'm here, to live this life. We never touched, never spoke intimately of anything and yet I knew that here was a possible future. I think she felt it, too.

The intrigue I feel about this woman is immense. I have a compulsion to get inside her head, to know everything. Being with her is one continuous déjà vu. Something about her touches me in a way I've never been touched before. I almost believe that if I were to close my eyes and concentrate enough, I could talk to her now, wherever she may be. I feel alive and vibrant. I feel I am.

Can feeling this much be wrong? Where is this going?

Sunday 12th November

I am a stranger in a strange land. I haven't really felt this before. Now that the novelty is beginning to wear off, the non-stop party appears to be stopping and the weather has turned nasty, I find I am questioning myself. What am I doing here? I feel the holiday is over and I need to make some decisions about what I'm going to do with my life. This would be a very easy place to just drift along in. I can well imagine looking back and finding three years gone by and my having achieved nothing. I'm going to make a more concerted effort with the Greek lessons. I don't actually know any real Greeks, Spiros aside - that should be my aim.

Do I miss England? No, not at all.

Why am I stocktaking my life all of a sudden? There is something serious going on here and I'm not at all sure what it is or whether I like it.

Is there a future out there?
To gaze unquestioning into the future
Is the pastime of fools
But to map and plan
Without rules
Is the bigger sin
Living live retrospectively
The 'to-come' can be ignored
Until too little remains
And still no roots have been forged
Pushed on again
Decisions have to be made
Can you marry your thoughts
And your desires
To stay the incessant haunts?
Commit yourself
Take hope in love… Forever.

I don't know where those last two lines came from.

I think I think too much.

Monday 13th November

I think I drink too much. Another horrendous day in work with a hangover. Richard is entirely to blame. He came round for curry last night and found a bottle of Cutty Sark under the sink. I had no idea it was there. It isn't any more. Curry and whiskey. My breath must have smelt great this morning; I'm surprised the kids weren't passing out. We thrashed out a couple of R.E.M. numbers on the guitar and there was talk of a song or two at the end of term bash next month.

Tuesday 14th November

Received a postcard from Rachel today. She's found a job and is tolerating living at home again, for now.

Which reminds me, my post from England is drying up. People seem to have stopped writing. I'm going to go through my address book alphabetically and write to everyone in the next two weeks. I realise that I am a little bored these days and am looking for a distraction.

I have made a list of all the people I'm going to write to. By the time I finish, I will have written twenty six letters, not including family. Have decided that it's near enough to Christmas to include cards and wait until 1st December to post them.

Wednesday 15th November

Went for a coffee after work with Abigail. She took me to a little Greek place, not at all like the flash plastic-plant-and-smoked-glass places I've been to with other Brits. I had my first Greek coffee which I instantly liked, much to the satisfaction of the woman who served it. It's more grainy than standard ground coffee, and almost stupidly strong. I love the way it's served, boiled in an individual little pot, called a *briki,* and served in the tiniest of coffee cups.

It was fascinating listening to Abigail speak fluent Greek one moment and then turn to me to speak English. She tells me it took her six months to learn the language. I've been here three months and I can only stretch to 'hello', 'goodbye' and 'I'd like another beer, please'. Actually, 'please' doesn't seem to figure too much in Greek.

We ended up talking about compassion for oneself. I have no idea how. It's so good to talk about feelings and fears and have someone so readily understand. I suspect we are very similar in many respects.

I invited her out on Friday evening. She would only be drawn as far as, "We'll see..." She'll tell me in school tomorrow. Sometimes I feel I'm making headway, but at others I think maybe I'm imagining it. There I go, thinking again.

Thursday 16th November

I spent half an hour this afternoon watching for her, like some love-sick teenager. Pathetic. Got twenty seconds of her time for my trouble. She seemed like a different person, cold and distant. She doesn't think she can make it on Friday.

Thoroughly pissed off when I got in from school. Also thoroughly pissed on, as it rained the whole way back. I took off my clothes and wrung them out. Message on the machine from Abigail says, "How about doing something on Sunday? I'll ring you when I get off work."

Pissed off to ridiculously happy in ten seconds flat. Serious warning bells ring in my head. Sod them, what do they know?

Friday 17th November

Joanne, of all people, sent me a video of various comedy shows, so I spent yesterday evening watching "Have I got news for you?", "Red Dwarf", "A bit of Fry and Laurie" and "Clive Anderson Talks Back". You can't beat a good dose of real culture now and then. She also asked if I planned to come back to the UK for Christmas. I'm avoiding thinking about it.

I have no idea what we're going to do on Sunday - just looking forward to spending some more time with Abigail.

I have been invited to a fondue evening tonight. Various people from school are going. Could be fun.

Saturday 18th November

Wasn't fun. Very formal and polite. It was like an extension of the working day. Lesson learned, won't do that again. A few of us left early and hit the usual haunts in town. The usual haunts are beginning to depress me. I need something new in my life. Am going to try to drink less and to keep fit. Did ten push-ups and thirty sit-ups today. Plan to do more tomorrow.

Sunday 19th November

A watched phone never rings... It's midday and I'm waiting for Abigail to call. I could call her, but for some reason I feel I shouldn't. So much for not playing games. So, I am writing to distract myself. I still haven't started any of my letters home; perhaps I should be doing that now. I'm not going to fall into the American-TV-series trap of a Sunday afternoon!

I can't get the idea out of my head that my existence here in Greece is empty. I need something concrete to do, to feel I am growing and achieving something. Teaching is always OK once the classroom door is closed, but these are privileged kids and I don't feel I have anything to offer them. I feel I am effectively an automaton, following a route with these kids which anyone could follow. The honourable and decent thing to do would be to quit and try to find something more worthwhile to do. However, the honourable and decent thing doesn't pay my pension, my rent and stash money away in the bank. (I'm twenty-eight, and I'm concerned about my pension?) I have no idea why I want to stash money away in the bank. To do what with? I don't want to buy a house, because I don't want to be tied to any one place. The eating-out-and-drinking-in-smart-bars lifestyle is seriously beginning to bore me. I'd like to get to know a Greek village, to live a lifestyle which is closer to nature, to drink ouzo and retsina with real Greeks, not the *nouveau riche* set. I do believe there's a reason I'm here now, a purpose for this life of mine. Just need to find out what it is!

EVENING. Abigail eventually phoned at two, asking if I was still free to do something. Like I hadn't been waiting since eight this morning , like I hadn't even left the house in case I missed her call! Didn't tell her this, of course.

Spooky coincidence: she wanted to get out of Kifissia and go somewhere more rural. Did I fancy lunch in a village in the mountains? Did I ever! We drove up towards the Basiliko Kipo, which means 'The King's Estate', or something like that. I had no idea that I was so close to such wilderness. This is an immense area of pine forests and stunted shrubs, which evidently a lot of people use for hunting. It's the typical Mediterranean scrubland I learnt about in Geography. Good to know some of it was on the mark. You can actually smell the wild herbs, particularly basil and something reminiscent of garlic. We drove along dirt roads for ages, quietly taking in the views. We finally arrived at a village called Kiurka, where we found a taverna and had Greek salad and chips. Abigail discovered that I didn't eat meat and found this a totally alien concept. The woman who served us was also confused by it, if not actually offended. People around us were ordering meat by the kilo: this is not an exaggeration.

She detected my mood, and we talked a lot about feeling a need to do something worthwhile, and not to prostitute my services in a cause I don't believe in. Her response was simple. If you're truly unhappy doing what you're doing now, then stop it. Nothing is so important as to demand your unhappiness. Let go, turn around and do something else. The only thing keeping you doing something you don't like is fear and uncertainty about the future. She sees fear as a challenge and uncertainty as an adventure. I owe it to myself to be true to how I feel and to live my life as I see fit. No-one, she tells me, is going to do that for me! Hmmm.

She, too, is very frustrated in her work: too few nurses, too few resources and a money-led waiting system seemed to be top of her list of grievances.

I plucked up the courage to ask her why she was so curt on the phone when I rang her on Friday. It turns out that she doesn't live alone. Warning bells tinkling softly again? Bloody clanging deafeningly, more like. It was a real effort of will not to hear them. After all, we're not having an affair here. This is a coffee-and-conversation relationship, and what we're doing is okay. I asked if he knew she was here. She didn't want to talk about him. Clearly things are not going well.

This is my cue to walk away. No nasty messy emotional entanglements, remember? Walk away while I still can, before this woman gets under my skin. Before it's too late. Before I have to admit that I'm falling in love. Oh, fuck.

She has just phoned to say thank you for a wonderful afternoon. She sounded so down. I wanted to be able to reach down and cure her pain. I want so much to help - but the intensity of her fundamental sadness is difficult to bear. But I know that today I have met someone who I have wanted to meet for a long time, perhaps forever. Sophisticated is too strong a word, but she is something that that is. Intelligent, certainly, with a way of thinking that I can't quite get to grips with, and yet which excites me and draws me in. Mature? I don't know. Certainly she has experienced a lot of life - but the obvious hints, the blatant retreats, raised shutters? Is this maturity? I don't think so, and yet I am intrigued by everything about her. I have never felt so cut off from someone I am talking to. She pulls me into her just so far, and then throws up her defences. It's so frustrating, her walls are everywhere. Do I really want to do this? Do I have a choice any more?

Not surprisingly, in this contemplative mood, no sit-ups or push-ups.

Monday 20th November

...or today.

Tuesday 21st November

...or today. So much for my super fitness regime. I'm having problems keeping interested at work. When I let go of the planning and recording side of it and focus on the classroom and the children, I have to admit that I enjoy specific moments of the day. The children amuse me and we do have fun.

I am definitely thinking too much. Am going to resort to pizza, alcohol and mindless TV with Richard tonight to try to stop it!

Wednesday 22nd November

I am completely uninspired. Haven't really seen Abigail since Sunday - only once very briefly in school. She looks very troubled. Why? I am going to try to write something for her.

Friday 24th November

There was a message on my answer machine last night when I got home. "Thank you for your letter. I don't know what else to say. I'm not going to be around for a few days, I have to get away. I'll ring you when I get back. Don't be sad: I just need time for me."

Fitness idea totally out of the window. Went out and bought four bottles of cheap white wine and tried to drink them all. Managed three.

Here I am, not being sad. Feel that to get through the next few days will be very hard.

Am worried that I am becoming obsessive.

Saturday 25th November

Friday night was a repeat of so many Friday nights here. Kept me busy though.

Today I shall go shopping and then cook something delicious for Richard and Renata, who are coming round at eight. Must also buy more wine. Am trying to think positively about this situation. Have even done sit-ups and push-ups today. Managed fifty of the former, only twelve of the latter. Still, it's an improvement.

Sunday 26th November

I believed myself incapable of loving another person. I believed that I had become cold and heartless. I had become the one who hurts in order not to be hurt. I had become the one who self-protects at all costs, who avoids commitment, who can only take. Harsh, but true. I did feel something for Rachel, but as soon as she had gone….a big nothing. The tears were tears of self-pity, I think. Feeling alone and lost.

Now I find myself thinking all the time about Abigail and wondering where she is, how she is. She told me last week that she is considering leaving Greece - my heart nearly stopped. Nobody would miss her, she told me. I told her I would. I told her I'd consider that a travesty, a personal disaster. She looked surprised. "You don't know me," she said. I know her better than she thinks: she's too much like me. She's really fucked up. Now I'm scared that her needing time to be alone actually means she's left Greece. Am I going to see her again? What am I going to do if I don't; or if I get a call saying she's in France?

Fearing the solitude of restless wakefulness, and wanting to be able to crash out instantly, I have in the past reached for a bottle. Tonight, I'm trying for exhaustion through exercise. I have just returned from a cycle ride up Pendeli. Actually Richard and I have done this a few times now. Coming down was exhilarating, and for a few minutes, it felt really good just to be alive. I am now doing sit ups and push ups in front of the telly. Richard instantly negates any exercise with beer, but I resist joining him.

Monday 27th November

Definitely overdid the exercising yesterday. I ache in places I didn't know I had places.

No telephone call. Tried her number: no answer.

Tuesday 28th November

No telephone call. Tried her number. Greek voice answered. Hung up.

Here I am, still not being sad!

Wednesday 29th November

In a supreme effort of will and purpose, I have written seven letters to friends in the UK over the last two days. I have until Friday evening to complete all twenty six. I shall have to sacrifice diary entries while work is in progress.

Saturday 2nd December

Still no phone call. My insides are squirming. I feel physically sick. The thought that she might not come back terrifies me. Why so strong?

I have to admit minor defeat on the letters front. In the interests of making them long enough and interesting enough to be worth receiving, I cut eight names off the list. They'll just get cards instead. Still, eighteen letters in four days is not at all bad. Have also written another long one to Abigail; I only hope I get to give it to her personally. I have an ominous feeling about what is happening here.

I must fight this feeling that I would be lost without her. It sounds crazy, I know am obsessing here. That's the nature of obsession – I can't help myself. Am I so sure that she is the direction I am looking for in life? I know that it is wrong to pin your expectations of happiness on another person. I know that being in love is a phase, not a reality. I know she cannot be the person I now believe her to be. I know she cannot be the answer to my demons. I know all these things, yet I feel so much that I want her to be the answer and the place I am heading towards, my reason for being.

Affirmation of self

Here, in what and where I am,
Reality, in all its forms does dwell
Now, in what I do and feel, I am alive.
Tomorrow, in fears and hopes, lives ahead
Ahead, with its twists and turns, is not fixed
Life, the learning and the growing, is this.
Being, honestly and fairly, is my goal,
Growing, to be the best that I can be, is my aim,
Success, in whatever form it takes, equals contentment.
It is me, myself, my relationship with me
That counts towards the person I want to be
The future me.
In this, no other person,
No outside force of love or support
Can equal the strength of my belief in myself.

Sunday 10th December

I have been working like a drone all week. Reports for all the kids plus loads of inconsequential internal paperwork that nobody will read anyway. Frustrating isn't the word.

Still no call from Abigail and actually I'm a bit pissed off about it now. It really wouldn't have hurt her just to let me know she's OK. Her absence has probably done me good, though. I feel I have got myself back into perspective a little. I don't need someone else around to feel good about myself - it's a hell of a lot easier that way, but not essential! (I won't admit, beyond these pages, that I have twice been down to the hospital car park when I know her shift ends, and her car is nowhere to be seen.)

I went cycling around Syngrou Park with Richard again today. I am absolutely knackered, but it is getting easier. Still resisted the proposed beer and felt good about it.

Monday 11th December

This is the last week in school this year. It's become really Christmassy! This is one of the things I really do like about teaching; Christmas with five year olds is what it's all about! We've stopped actually working, and have been making cards and calendars and table decorations. It's a bit like a production line at times, but all the kids get a bagful of goodies to take home at the end of term. I remember very proudly taking toilet-roll crackers and a very dodgy table decoration home when I was at school.

Went to the hospital again after work. I got up the nerve to go in and ask if she was working. She'd been ill, I was told.

Tuesday 12th December

Abigail has been staying with a friend not two kilometres from my flat! She says she's fine and would like to see me today, after school. No apology for not having phoned me though. She had a call from a friend at the hospital, saying that an English guy had been in looking for her. I'm so relieved to hear from her that my anger dissipates into thin air the second I hear her voice. She's been 'on the sick' from work but will be in from tomorrow. She's coming round in an hour or so. I have some manic tidying up to do.

Finally, the look is held - but too long. She is trying to see something in me. Why? What is her interest? My hand reaches for hers. I need to touch her. I need to feel that she is real. Her hand in mine now, no retreat, but little response. What is she thinking? I find myself saying things to her that, normally, I would hide only in the pages of a notebook. I am disarmed. I am trusting. I am hoping for understanding and (here comes the amazing truth) I do not feel scared. I am not afraid of this person; I do not fear her responses. I perhaps fear her disapproval, but I love her honesty.

She sits with me, her hands in mine, intertwining, exploring. She looks sad, silent: empty looks telling me she is not here at all. I feel her angst and despair; I recognise these things as I recognise her numbness, her inability to feel. Why do I care so much, and how? I didn't think I could.

The backs of my fingers against her face now, caressing her cheek. Her eyes half close, almost giving in to the moment, almost trusting the sensation, almost letting go, almost…The intense look, the silent withdrawal, shutters up. She needs so much to be in control. She has released me though, from my own similar fate. Whilst I begin to feel alive again, able to love again, she feels only sadness, with an intensity which scares me. I tell her so, she says nothing. She is cold, distant, afraid, but doesn't want to be any of those things.

I am sure my intuition here has been right. But do I really want to do this, only to discover that she has to leave? Am I strong enough for two? Until today, I still didn't believe that I was strong enough for one. And I owe her that. I feel that I am at the edge of a new beginning. And now, I sit here writing, the last few hours spent quietly in thought, thoughts exclusively of her. Her thoughts, her hands so confused, her body language, her ideas, her expectations, a mass of contradictions. Underneath it all, I think she wants to open up, but she doesn't want to need someone. She's been there.

My life has changed, whatever happens next. And tonight, with her in my head, I have come to know myself better.

Wednesday 13th December

She told me last night that she could make no promises to me. She felt that any involvement would simply be her using me. She felt drawn to me, certainly attracted, wanted to sleep with me, wanted to know me, but wanted to be on her own. She doesn't know what she wants. That's okay; I'm sure enough for the both of us. I don't want promises for the future. The future scares the Hell out of me. I want her, now, in the present and the future can take care of itself. For too much of my life I have been pre-occupied with the past, feeling guilty for things I can no longer influence, or worried about the future, which I am equally powerless to predict. It is time to learn to concentrate on my 'now', and to be happy in what I'm doing, when I'm doing it. When I think of the opportunities I've missed in my life through worrying about what might be, or what I might miss… What a waste!

She's going to look for a new flat after Christmas. She's going to go to Paris at Christmas.

Christmas… Not for the first time it occurs to me that I have to make plans of my own. I don't feel at all that I miss England and need to go and visit anyone there. I suppose I'll do that though - I can't imagine staying here. This temporary community packs its bags and flies the coup for the holiday season.

Christmas isn't really a big deal here - you can walk through the streets of Athens and not know it's mid-December. This is strange coming, as I do, from a country which is increasingly trying to look like mid-December from the beginning of September. Apparently the Greeks go a bundle on Easter though, being soundly Orthodox and all that.

Managed to book a ticket to Manchester for the 20th.

Thursday 14th December

Last full day in school, as tomorrow we finish at midday. Waste of time trying to do anything constructive. We sat the kids in front of "Santa Claus -The Movie" for a couple of hours while we began stripping the decorations. Then into the hall for a chaotic and migraine-inducing 'party'. Exhausting, but fun.

After I got in, sweating and tired from my bike ride up the hill, Abigail came around. She wanted to thank me for my letter. She wanted to know how I could trust my feelings about her. She hoped I wasn't expecting anything from her, not even that she would be back after the Christmas break. Said she couldn't stay long as she had to be in for the night shift in a couple of hours. Everything she says with words denies what she feels with her body. The pure sensual and spiritual pleasure I get from just touching her face is beyond any feeling I'd ever imagined. I know she experiences this too. I kissed her once, as she was leaving. I am floating. As she left, she said, "You make me melt." I took that as a compliment. I pulled her back to me, but she resisted, trying to hide the tears welling in her eyes. Ding-a-ling-a-ling!

Friday 15th December

Last day today. Richard and I are going in to work wearing Bermuda shorts and jackets and ties. Comments were made about maintaining professional dress, so someone has to test the limits. Someone has to make an effort!

Saturday 16th December

Teachers always get presents from the kids at the end of this term, but here it is like nothing I've ever experienced before. I had a case of twelve bottles of wine from one family, a solid silver key fob from another and a set of two huge beach towels from another! I'm not a chocolate fan, so the mass of chocolates and sweet things will go to other more appreciative recipients over the next few days. The bottles have found their spiritual home though.

Abigail came in for the end of term bash at school - she looked knackered and had clearly come straight from work. She sat next to me at the buffet, and it was exasperating not to be able to touch her. She seemed happy to stay, especially as a couple of the teachers were now playing guitars and piano. When we did leave, it was great to see her face light up in the car when I showed her all the chocolate stuff I'd been given and asked if she wanted any of it. It sounds ridiculous now, but I could live a lifetime on that moment. The vague sadness in her eyes disappeared and they lit up her face. It was the first time I'd seen her nearly laugh. God, to be able to see this woman smile each morning: that's really all I ask out of life!

We went to another colleague's flat for pizza and a video. Lucked out with the video though; it was good, but very black and thoroughly depressing. I found myself feeling protective of Abigail and not wanting her to watch it. Careful. I must try not to crowd her. As she sat next to me on the sofa, it was unbearable to feel unable to reach out for her. She must have felt something too, because the one time we found ourselves alone in the room, she turned to me and gave me the most tender and heartfelt of kisses, accompanied by a look that seemed to see into my heart.

We arrived back at my flat at mid-night. We'd had a glass of wine at Julie's place, but I certainly wanted another. So, as she was helping me get my various carrier bags and the crate of wine out of the car, I asked her if she'd like to help me test the vintage.

We managed to sit and talk for hours. She seemed amused by my attentiveness towards her - I couldn't keep my hands off her. To feel her fingers entwined in mine, to feel the smoothness of her face against the backs of my fingers, to feel the warmth of her lips against my finger-tips: I was sure that making love could only be an anti-climax to these sensations.

I was wrong about that.

I woke at five-thirty, to see her dressed and trying to leave the room without making the door squeak.

"Hey, you're going?" I asked lamely.

"I have to. See you soon." This so warmly that I couldn't feel anything but elated. With that she leant over me, gave me a kiss that thoroughly woke me up, and then left.

I am stupidly spending all day at home today hoping she'll ring. It's now seven-thirty in the evening and I've just turned down an invitation from the whole crowd who are going into Athens. I couldn't enjoy anyone else's company just now. I'd only be wishing I were with her, wondering if she was trying to call me.

Sunday 17th December

She wasn't. I sat in alone all evening with the TV and some excellent Irish whiskey. All my paranoia screaming through my head: what if she's regretting it, what if it was a last fling in Greece before she leaves, what if, what if, what if…? Get a grip! What if I fall under a bus tomorrow, what if I get fired, what if I get cancer, what if Plymouth Argyle win the FA Cup? Who gives a fuck? Now; now; now! It's my 'now' that counts!

It is bizarre. Nothing rational bodes well for this relationship, only the strength of feeling I have. It is something right. It is something to do with why I'm here. It is something to do with my becoming the person I keep aiming to be, and keep falling dismally short of realising. Before meeting her, I didn't believe I could ever let anyone near me again. Now I can't get close enough.

I do believe in myself. I believe that my faith in my intuition has been well placed. Whether or not a future can be moulded from this present, I am so much a better person for her company. I feel anger, jealousy and confusion - powerful emotions I thought I had lost. I feel trust, hope and maybe even love - stronger still, and more deeply lost. I want to understand and to know her. I want to hold her when she cries. I want to be reflected in her eyes when she laughs. I want to be the person she turns to with her hopes, her worries, her joy, her despair. I want to be able to watch and smile inside as she talks to other people - proud and happy that she is choosing to be with me. Do I want too much?

Of course I do - that's the nature of the beast. I hope that one day she knows what she wants, and that I can be at least a part of it.

Monday 18th December

I really did expect a call yesterday. Nothing. Until I went out for ten minutes to buy some milk from a kiosk. I came back to two messages answer machine. The first was from Abigail: "Oh, God, I hate talking to these things. Sorry I had to leave like that. I hadn't planned to stay at all. Can I see you tomorrow? Give me a ring."

I resisted the temptation to phone straight away and needlessly explain that she had just missed me.

The second message was from Rachel. "This is going to sound stupid, but I'm going to say it anyway, while I still have the nerve. You said you didn't have plans for Christmas. I know it's last minute and it might be expensive, but how would you like to come out to Taz for Christmas? Think about it. Call me."

I waited an hour before calling Abigail, only to find she'd gone out. Her friend said she didn't know how long she'd be and that she'd ask her to call me. Bollocks! I should have called back straight away!

Shallow and superficial as I am, Rachel's offer suddenly seems enticing too. Why not? Actually, there are lots of reasons why not.

I left the flat early this morning, to go Christmas shopping for the kids of the friends I will be seeing in England. I was determined not to wait in all day for a call. I found nothing that impressed me and was returning almost empty-handed, when a car beeped behind me. Abigail leaned out of the window and offered me a lift home. Home was about ten yards away at this point.

She took me to a huge toy store and helped me choose all my presents in no time at all. She even helped to wrap them when we got back home. No speech about having made a mistake, or 'the other night was great but…' There was, for now though, clearly going to be no repeat performance. She had been and collected some of her things from her flat and was to fly to France in the morning. No, she couldn't stay tonight; she had to leave at five a.m. This story sounded frighteningly familiar to me, and I wondered briefly at its significance. I didn't push the point, although I did say that our timing was lousy and that I'd miss her over Christmas. No reciprocal declarations, I noticed, but then what right had I to expect them?

Her flight back arrives on 3rd January, a Wednesday. Mine's the day after. I have her number in France, but she says she'll be moving around a lot. She also didn't ask for mine.

Saying goodbye to her felt like saying goodbye forever. I am not going to spend my entire holiday wondering what's going on. I will call her once, and once only.

Tuesday 19th December

Richard and I were booked on the same flight tomorrow. Actually, not that huge a coincidence given that we work in the same school and live in the same country. We had planned to leave here at midnight tonight, meeting in Kifissia for Richard to drink enough beer to overcome his flight-phobia. Sounded like a good plan a very few days ago. Now I shall have to lie to my best friend, and claim, unconvincingly I'm sure, that I've decided to stay put for the holidays.

Wednesday 20th December

7am. Athens International Airport. Actually feeling quite unwell following my night out with Richard last night, who, incidentally, wasn't in the least bit surprised or put out that I'd opted to stick around. I almost told him my plans; it felt so wrong lying to him. My Olympic Airways flight for Sydney, via Dubai, leaves in just over an hour, with a connecting flight to Hobart in about twenty-four hours from now. I am childishly excited about making this trip, and about seeing Rachel again. All sorts of emotions are fighting for supremacy. What am I doing?

Part Two

the epsilon, the mi and the pi

Sunday 17th March

A foundation,
And a security
Of love trusted and believed in.
A dawning,
A growing awareness,
Of new and powerful possibilities.
A memory
Repressed
Of love and hopes dashed apart.
A hope,
Glimmering belief,
That together we can do this differently
A certainty,
A profound knowledge,
That we will go grow in the trying.
Courage again,
Setting adrift
In the unpredictable tide of a new life.
Fear again,
Of course,
At abandoning the known.
An eruption,
A thrill inside,
At living a life worthy of ourselves.
Belief again,
Clarity,
As we rise out of our ordinary existence.
Ecstasy,
Serenity,
As we begin to realise and achieve our true potential.

We drove to Loutraki, across the Corinth Canal, and contrary to weather forecasts of rain and cold, found glorious sunshine and the blossoming of spring. The canal crossing is truly impressive, made all the more memorable by my leaning over and losing my sunglasses into the chasm. We walked arm in arm along the pebbled beach and spoke to one another in the silence of thought. So often now, words seem unnecessary, inadequate even, to say what we need to say to each other. The silences, the looks we exchange and the knowing are so much more powerful than any words we might use. Paradise found.

My first foray into the Mediterranean! This is March, and I'm strolling casually through the tiny waves breaking on the shore! We sat on the beach, holding each other, and for me the world stopped again. I find myself experiencing such sheer bliss that I cannot imagine anything or anybody else existing. For these moments, we are all that there is, all that there will be, all that matters. Other things in my life drift away and pale into insignificance. Intense and complete, my love for her has become the greater part of my life. I know that this is dangerous, but I'm tired of running from danger. Not this time; I know what I want and I'm going to put everything I have into getting it.

We arrived home tired but happy. Tomorrow morning I will again have to face reality, and leave her half sleeping in bed as I go to work. Leaving her each morning is the hardest part of my day. Stepping back into our illusional but perfect world each afternoon is the thought that gets me through it. Losing ourselves in each other, cutting off the outside, intertwining physically and spiritually, willing the world to stop now, for this moment to go on and on and on...

And as I relish what I have found, the warning bells still ring and cause me to fear for the future. Love must not become need...

> *Sensibilities slowly attune to their surroundings*
> *Unconsciousness drifts towards consciousness*
> *And the sub-reality of REM sleep*
> *Evolves into awareness*
> *For a tantalising few micro-seconds*
> *Dreams co-exist with lucidity*
> *Before the structures of logic*
> *Impose reality upon beauty*
> *And it dies.*

Monday 18th March

Came back from work today to find Abigail not home, which isn't unusual. Since I persuaded her to come back to Greece and to move in with me here, she has been looking for work. She has a few lessons teaching French and is looking for more. I sometimes find a note, or something half-cooked in the oven. But today - nothing.

Our interminable phone calls in January and February always came back to a theme: how could she come back to Greece solely on the strength of her feelings for me? That would put immense pressure on the relationship to work, and almost guarantee that it wouldn't. She needed to want to come back for herself. She no longer had a job out here. She also knew that she had nothing in France to stay for and I thought staying there was just avoidance. I'd told her so and she never once denied it. We spent hours going over the same ground.

We also spent hours going over my somewhat impulsive trip to Australia. What was I thinking? Was I sure about how I felt now? Why did I come back? At times, it was all too tiring and complicated for her to contemplate. I know that she was often close to simply washing her hands of it all. My own ambivalence there probably didn't help. At least now I'm clearer about what I want. I do have to admit that this is due more to Rachel's maturity than my own. Loving someone turns out to be not at all what I thought it was all about.

We agreed in the end that Abigail would come and live with me on the understanding that as soon as she was financially set up, she would find a place of her own and we would see what we would see... Even so, I had to go to France to get her. I have had more than my fair share of airports and jetlag these last few months.

I love being here when she's not around - not because I don't like her being around, quite the contrary. But when she's not here, I feel her presence in the books on the shelves, the clothes in the cupboards (and strewn around the flat), the selection of obscure ethnic and esoteric classical CD's, the empty espresso cup that wasn't there when I left this morning and her cello in its stand in the corner of the lounge. I find myself deliriously happy in the thought that she is here, has chosen to be with me, that she is the last person I see before I go to sleep at night and the first person I see on waking in the morning. I even pinch myself from time to time...

Tuesday 19th March

The temporary sunny spell has subsided and we are in the midst of winter again. I cannot believe how cold it can be in this country. I remember the numbing coldness of student digs in England, I remember getting off the train in Blackpool one Christmas to a temperature of -10°C, but 5 or 6 degrees in Athens feels positively Arctic. I wonder why this should be. Is it just a case of psychological expectations? I don't think so. When I cycled to school this morning it certainly wasn't my head telling me that I'd lost all feeling in my nether regions! I think it may be partly due to the fact that nowhere in Greece has proper heating. You can be freezing in buildings which supposedly have working central heating, or you can be sat in a café heated solely by an ineffectual portable gas heater. School is a mixture: at one end, where the heating system begins, it is unbearably hot - even necessitating the opening of windows at times this winter, whilst upstairs the pipes and radiators range from tepid to stone cold. And once you get cold, it seems to take forever to get warm again. I haven't resorted to wearing anything in bed yet, but getting up in the morning in February in Athens ranks with those memories of crawling from beneath a duvet into a room where you could see your breath and where the ice clung to the inside of the windows to attend morning lectures at university, when it was all too easy not to bother... Not bothering is not really an option any more.

Wednesday 20th March

Abigail has an interview tomorrow. Got home today and she'd cooked an extravagant meal for two, with wine and flowers and everything. I sometimes feel guilty feeling so good.

Found a kitten at school today. It seems that people quite often dump an unwanted animal here in the hope that a child will latch onto it during the day and then emotionally blackmail the parents into keeping it. Well, no emotional blackmail involved this time as I was the mug who found it. He's all black, except for four little white feet. We're going to call him Kaltsoula, which means 'little sock' (it definitely sounds better in Greek). He has established himself very quickly in the flat, and has proven already to be a vicious little git. I'm not sure his character is too good, but he looks extremely cute.

Thursday 21st March

Abigail has found a job, four mornings a week working at the French Institute in Athens. With her private lessons, she now has a survivable income. The decent and mature side of me, which I have been working extremely hard to promote in recent months, is overjoyed for her. It was this side which prompted me to splash out on Champagne etc. We are going out tomorrow to eat, drink and be merry.

The slightly seedy and less healthy side of me pointed out that now that she no longer needed me, from a financial point of view, she might leave. My mature side countered that this was only insecurity talking, but we should talk about it now that it is a possibility. Maybe it's something she'd like to do, to have space to herself, room to breathe? My seedy side convinced me that to broach the subject was to invite disaster. I don't like my seedy side all that much, but I have to concede that I think it's got a point. Things are going so well at the moment, why rock the boat? Why am I such an abject coward?

Kaltsoula has taken to hiding behind things and attacking me whenever I walk past him. It's an amusing game, until you step naked out of the shower…

Friday 22nd March

It has now been raining for twenty-four hours non-stop. I could literally canoe into work, had I such a thing. As I don't, I have to resort to the school bus, which passes tolerably close to my flat. Not having expected this weather when I first came to Greece, and not having thought about it whilst spending a sunny Christmas down under, I am without boots, without umbrella and without a decent coat of any description. I managed to borrow a bright yellow anorak, which, apart from looking ridiculous, leaks in various places. I arrived at school today in no state to teach, soaked from head to foot. I was ferried back home at eleven this morning, sneezing and shivering all the way in still damp clothes. I'm sat in bed, drinking hot lemon and honey, having raided the aspirins, and wondering what time Abigail will be home from her first day in work.

The cat is totally unimpressed with the weather and refuses to venture past the open door. I'm totally unimpressed with the cost of cat litter and cat food. It didn't occur to me that keeping a cat would be expensive. Now Abigail tells me that I have to find a vet and make sure the cat has all manner of injections.

Monday 25th March

We didn't go out to celebrate Abigail's new job on Friday, as I was asleep most of the evening. Didn't really feel much better until Sunday afternoon. The floods had subsided by then, so we drove up to Oropos, on the coast opposite Evia, and sat in the feeble sunshine at a waterfront taverna.

As Monday is the morning Abigail doesn't work, I took the day off. Beats working for a living.

Kaltsoula enjoys sitting at the foot of the bed and pouncing on anything that moves under the duvet. This can be very off-putting at times.

Tuesday 26th March

Returned to work today. I always feel slightly guilty about missing work, even when I am genuinely ill, feeling that colleagues will be put under undue pressure or that something won't work the way it should, or the way I would have wanted it to. It's crazy to think that way. I'm reminded of a few things: the lyrics from a song by Timbuk 3, *"It's just another jerk taking pride in his work"*. Harsh maybe, but often fitting. Also I read somewhere the other day that feeling indispensable in your place of work was one of the first signs of madness. And yet another story springs to mind. I can't think where it comes from. Is it Bach again? There's a man, worried about leaving his job to go on holiday. He agonises about whom to leave in charge and leaves precise instructions for everyone. He talks with an older man, a spiritual guru of some kind, an advisor, who draws him the following analogy: "Imagine yourself to be a brick in the ocean. When you are gone, such is the space you will leave behind." This stuck in my mind as the foundation of a philosophy of life!

Basically everything runs fine when I'm not there, which adds to my feeling that I'm not actually making any kind of difference, that my role is an unimportant one that any automaton could fill, that I should be doing something more worthwhile with my life.

Wednesday 27th March

Haven't really found anything more worthwhile to do with my life, so went to work again today.

Came home to the cat crying loudly at the fridge door. Tried to fob him off with some veggie left-overs, but he was having none of it. He is very assertive and demanding, and not in a nice way.

Sit-up and push-up regime still holding good, after nearly a month! Still supplemented by regular alcohol intake, so perhaps I'm not feeling the fullest benefit.

Thursday 28th March

Came home today to the strains of what I later discovered was the Prelude from the Bach's Suite No. 1 in G major, the first of his *Six Suites for Unaccompanied Cello.* A nice surprise – it has been a while since she picked it up.

We have been planning our Easter holiday. We have thought about going to France to stay with friends of Abigail's, but neither of us is particularly enthusiastic. We also considered going to an island - Easter is a big deal in Greece and apparently it's well worth seeing the celebrations. Some of the more religious islands do it very well, Abigail tells me. But they'll be very busy and I don't know how keen I am on the 'roasting-lambs-in-the-street' part.

Another option is to hire a car (Abigail's is too unreliable for us to risk the trip in it) and do a tour around a part of Sterea Ellada, mainland Greece, camping and finding rooms as we go. This appeals to me. We'll see. We've got a week to think about it. We have to find someone to feed Kaltsoula while we're away. Richard won't, because he's met him.

Friday 29th March

Abigail spent yesterday evening teaching me to play *tavli*, or what I would call backgammon. There are, apparently, three versions of the game which you are supposed to play one after the other, but she could only remember the first two. She beat me soundly for a few games, then got pissed off when I told her it was just a game of luck. If you rely on throwing dice, surely it's just luck? Maybe I'm just a bad loser! I tried to get her to learn chess, but she says she doesn't have the patience. Chess is a game requiring skill, which is perhaps why I'm not very good at it. (Well, I'm good enough to beat anyone who's got as far as knowing the moves, but once I meet someone who actually knows something about openings and long term strategies, I fall apart.)

We're going out tonight in belated celebration her new-found employment.

Saturday 30th March

We went to an Italian restaurant in Kifissia last night. What a performance! Abigail found something good to eat, but the vegetarian selection was decidedly slim, and I ended up having plain spaghetti which even I could have made more palatable. Every time we took more than a sip from either a wine or water glass, the waitress would materialise and re-fill it. It was most unnerving. I'm much happier being left totally alone as long as there's food and wine actually on the table. I suppose many of the people who eat here have servants and maids at home and so they're used to this kind of thing. It was the first time I had been waited on quite so enthusiastically; it was a distinctly uncomfortable experience.

The wine was marvellous though, and we finished the bottle only to have another arrive promptly in its place. I thought this was going over the top, and protested, only to find that it had been bought for us by a couple at the other end of the restaurant. As I looked up, I saw the parents of one of the kids in my class, and waved in grateful acknowledgement. Actually, I felt decidedly odd about it; I hadn't come out to feel beholden to someone else. I told Abigail how I felt. She said, "Fuck it". If they could afford it, it wasn't a problem. Either they were being genuinely thoughtful, in which case there was no problem, or they were trying to show off and parade their wealth, in which case they were twats and we'd take the wine anyway. No problem. I guess she was right.

Got home somewhat drunk and fell into bed. I still cannot find the words to describe how it is to make love to someone I love so much. There's something spiritual, something beyond the two people that we are: those moments when time stands still, and just being, in the 'now', is everything that I need. It's funny, when you try to manufacture these moments, they just don't work. Then, sometimes, they appear out of nowhere, and it's not just about sex. They can happen anytime, while we're doing the most basic and mundane things. The other day, while she was washing up, I stood behind her and held her, smelling her hair. She didn't stop what she was doing, and there was nothing sexual in the embrace. It was a snatched moment of perfection; a moment when just existing, totally centred in my 'now', was a sublime pleasure.

Spending today in the unwelcome trivia of real life: shopping, cleaning, tidying the flat, teaching the cat to use the litter tray. Existing is not always a sublime pleasure.

Sunday 31st March

We have decided to do the 'round-a-bit-of-Greece' thing, rather than venture abroad. I should have felt odd about going back to France, having only just been there to convince her to actually get on a plane and return to Greece. I still feel a little guilty about that, as I'm not sure she would have come had I not been so persistent. It was certainly what I wanted, but if ultimately it turns out to have been a mistake, she'll end up blaming me. Thoughts such as these, encroaching upon my imagined perfection, I usually shove to the back of my mind, and out altogether if I can. This one keeps returning though. The bastard.

A friend of Abigail's from the hospital has agreed to feed the cat. She hasn't met him yet.

Monday 1st April

April Fool's Day in school. Always good for a laugh, with the Secondary Section kids covering every conceivable surface with Vaseline. Very amusing. Sent Richard a convincing summons from the Head re-his woefully inadequate planning, and he was daft enough to be taken in by it. Today of all days. Reckons he owes me one. We shall see.

Also remembered today was, is, Joanne's birthday. Was tempted to call to wish her well, then decided against it. It wouldn't achieve anything apart from appeasing my conscience a little, which is hardly an honourable motive for calling someone on her birthday.

Tuesday 2nd April

At the end of school today, I found my bicycle up a tree, padlocked. Ha, ha, ha! Richard had made an early escape from school, so no key. He'll be pissed off tomorrow when he finds that I have sawn through his new bike chain! What did he think I would do? I have also chosen not to mention the incident, and so give no kudos thereby.

Wednesday 3rd April

I have called the car hire company and booked a Nissan Micra for Sunday morning. Now all we need to do is work out where we want to go. The weather's not great, nor is the forecast, but we'll make the best of whatever comes along. I hope I'm not expecting too much!

I pinch myself again to think I am going away for two weeks with this woman! Hell, she lives with me now, and I still can't quite accept it! I must get a grip; I deserve to be this happy! I'm a nice guy, why shouldn't I feel good? Why do I keep questioning it?

Kaltsoula has done a runner. He insisted on being let out this morning when I left for school and now there's no sign of him. Abigail says she hasn't seen him all day.

Thursday 4th April

Still no sign of the cat. I even checked around the streets near us to see if he'd met an untimely end under a Greek vehicle's tyres. Not that I could tell. Abigail has been calling him on and off all day, which I think is a total waste of time as he never once paid the slightest bit of attention when we tried to teach him his name. He didn't come to the sound of a spoon banging his bowl either, though, which is weird: self-centred and gutsy little creature that he is (was?).

Friday 5th April

My second term of teaching in Greece finally draws to a close. Only my second term? It seems like I've been here a lifetime already. Would I even recognise the person I was when I arrived less than seven months ago? An uneventful close of term it was too. Received eleven assorted Easter eggs though, which Abigail was happy about.

Kaltsoula has still not returned. Can't say I miss the little bastard much. I still have smarting scratches down the backs of my legs from his early morning attack on the day he disappeared.

The weather continues to worsen: it's cold and windy and no fun at all on a push-bike.

Sunday 7th April

Spent most of yesterday cleaning the house, prior to leaving later today. We thought we heard Kaltsoula a couple of times, but they were false alarms. Oh well.

We intend heading east along the south coast of the Sterea Ellada (Mainland Greece), and following the coast roads as far as we can before turning North into Epirus, where we plan to visit Ioannina, The Vikos Gorge and Metsova. Maybe on the way back we will be able to visit The Meteora, an apparently spectacular array of monasteries, built on the tops of precipitous pinnacles of rock (they were the setting for a James Bond film, I seem to remember, but I'm not sure which one). Well, this is the plan…

Monday 8th April

After we had been on the road for about forty minutes, Abigail suddenly thought she might have left the water heater on at home. That was a great start.

She hadn't, which made having gone back all the more irksome.

We drove along the National Road as far as Thebes and then cut across to Livadia. There seemed to be little cause to stop there, particularly given the appalling weather. We drove on and passed through Arachova, which looks like a beautiful little village. It perches on the edge of the mountain, Parnassos, and is a popular ski resort. No skiing today though. Maybe some white water rafting! Just outside of Arachova is the ancient site of Delphi. We again decided not to bother stopping as, even in such appalling weather, there were bus-loads of tourists streaming in and out of the site. It's crazy: there is only one narrow road, and yet there must have been twenty or so coaches parked alongside it. The traffic was mildly chaotic. This is definitely somewhere I'd like to come back to, though.

To the accompaniment of the pounding rain, we arrived in Galaxidi, which must be beautiful in the sunshine. It's a cute little fishing port, a little given over to tourism, but still retaining its charm. We ate here, and then argued playfully about who was going to drive. I won.

Since the rain didn't stop, neither did we. We drove all the way to Nafpaktos, which, although only about sixty kilometres away, takes a good couple of hours to reach. The map doesn't show the tortuous bends and horrendously steep climbs. We arrived with the fading light, and I was dispatched to ask for rooms. I think Abigail thinks that she is helping me to use my Greek by sending me off to do stuff like this. I'd rather she just did it herself, since she can. I guess she's right though, and that I'm just being lazy. I found us a great room, with pleasant views of the coast from the balcony. I could learn to live like this. What's to learn?

It's going to be cold tonight without any heating. We raided the room next door, which is not occupied, and 'stole' the extra blankets from the cupboard. We have a small bottle of ouzo too. I'm sure we'll find something to do to keep warm...

Tuesday 9th April

We have driven all day, and are staying in a place called Preveza. Very pretty, but I'm beginning to feel all pretty-villaged out. Too much driving in one day for my liking, but there's not much else to do with the weather being so fucking abysmal. We are wet and tired and retiring to bed early.

The weather report on the radio says tomorrow will be bright and sunny! Not! Our gorge walk in Papingo is out if this keeps up.

Wednesday 10th April

Having more-or-less by-passed Arta yesterday, we decided to go back and visit today. Although it isn't actually raining, you wouldn't call it a glorious day. Arta has an apparently famous footbridge, made entirely from local stone. It is impressive, with its huge arch across the Arathos River.

But for all its history and ancient sites, nothing has touched me as much as the enormous tree we found by the bridge. Its girth must have been six or seven metres, its limbs so huge and heavy that they are supported by wooden scaffolding in places. I couldn't have guessed an age, beyond hundreds of years. I discovered from one local that it was a one thousand year old plane tree, and, I was impressed to discover, is a preserved natural monument. I didn't think they lived to be so old. Another local, as if confirming my doubts, told us it was a sycamore, which was used to hang Greeks during the Ali Pasha's bloody reign. I find myself wondering what it has seen, this ancient sentinel. Did it witness the rise and fall of the great city states, like Sparta and Troy? It survived four hundred years of Turkish rule and two World Wars. For me this has a more real sense of history than the ancient masonry so expansively and universally revered.

It was too early to settle somewhere for the day and we wanted to push on further, so we headed north to Ioannina, as the rain began again. Arriving at midday, we looked around a little, but the driving rain and the freezing wind put us off a bit. Two old guys were trying to sell us a boat trip to a little island in the lake: not bloody likely! It also proved an expensive place to stay. We asked in a couple of hotels, but they charged ridiculous amounts and were not particularly inviting. We have decided to do some more driving and head north again; this time towards Papingo.

Thursday 11th April

Mikro Papingo. What an incredible place! Driving here and finding this village is how I imagined, as a kid, it would be to find Brigadoon. Tucked away in the mountains, hidden by cloud and rock, this is a spectacularly beautiful, if very wet, place. We had taken a guide book for walking in the area, and had planned to do a four and a half hour trek around the two villages of Mikro (small) Papingo and Megalo (big) Papingo, to Drakolimni (Dragon Lake). The book is full of delightful sounding walks and hikes, but none of them had this kind of weather in mind, I think. It is bitterly cold, feeling as though it is going to snow! For the moment it just rains and rains. We abandoned our plans to walk today and just roamed around the village.

It's more-or-less a purpose-built tourist resort and instantly reminds me of Ambleside in the Lake District, but considerably smaller. There can't be more than thirty or so houses here. The stone houses are full of charm and in one of them we found an exquisite little room, wood-panelled with a huge bed and an open fire. I'm amazed we made it out of the room at all…

Hospitality is not dead, even here where they expect tourists. Having discovered that I was a teacher, the proprietor of the taverna where we ate lunch all but sat himself down at our table and ate with us! He was impressed, for some reason, and insisted that we have a carafe of his retsina, on the house. We, in turn, promised to return in the evening to sample his meat-free dishes. He also said that this was the wettest and coldest Easter he could remember. No comment.

Friday 12th April

It's a little expensive here, and not particularly authentic 'Greek', but the mountains are spectacular and the fresh air is so sweet you can almost taste it.

Saturday 13th April

We left the mountains and the worst of the rain behind us this morning as we headed back towards Ioannina. We pretty much just passed through again, stopping only long enough to root around in a few little antique/jewellery-type shops. We visited the Perama caves, just outside Ioannina, apparently used as a hiding place by locals in 1940 during Nazi occupation. They are impressive, if you like caves. It's not Cheddar Gorge though.

Sunday 14th April

We stayed in Perama last night at a really grotty little hotel-cum-bed-and-breakfast place. It was all we could find, and was intensely disappointing after our homely room of the past three nights. The one saving grace was the old woman who owned the place, who insisted on telling us the story of Ali Pasha, who ruled Ioannina at the end of the eighteenth century. She told the story, in Greek, to Abigail as though it had happened last week to a close personal friend of hers. He was clearly not a very nice guy, having drowned his son's wife and entourage at one point, because she wouldn't sleep with him. He was very friendly with the British at one stage (my being British having prompted this story), but he was finally executed by the Turks. His head was taken back to Constantinople for its final resting place, after having been paraded around the region. The old woman, whose name I couldn't even say, let alone spell, seemed to find this last part very amusing. It takes all sorts. I have the impression that the story was gorier and more debauched than this, but I only got Abigail's potted, translated version.

Today, we are heading for Metsova.

Monday 15th April

We have a dog! This was not meant to happen. It's like the cat thing all over again. A misplaced sense of responsibility for helpless animals. On the road to Metsova, climbing high in the Pindos Mountains, we came across a starved and bedraggled brown and white beagle-cum-pointer. She was a truly pathetic sight, dragging her back legs behind her as she manifestly couldn't use them. She mustn't have eaten for about a week; she was almost a skeleton. It was sleeting heavily by this time, rather then just raining, and the temperature was dropping noticeably; we were sure that if we were to leave her here, she would die. We managed to put her into the back of the car and to feed her the little bread we had with us. Two minutes of twisting mountain roads later, and she had thrown up all over the back seat. There's gratitude for you!

The plan was to take the dog to any nearby village where she was more likely to be fed and looked after. This was always a dubious plan, as the Greeks are not exactly animal lovers, at least not in any way that the English would recognise. Suffice to say, we ended up buying milk and a couple of tins of luncheon meat to feed her properly.

When we arrived in Metsova we had not only to find a room, but to find a room into which we could conceivably smuggle a dog. This actually proved very easy. The first place we tried was ideal. It was old, and far from plush, but had a great looking *somba*, a kind of a Darlek-shaped wood-burning stove. Abigail insisted that the dog could not stay in the car overnight, as she would probably freeze to death. So we wrapped her in a sleeping bag after dark, and snuck in with her. She's now fast asleep, next to the stove, dreaming happy doggy dreams. Abigail has gone out to buy her a *souvlaki*.

Tuesday 16th April

We had a chance to look around Metsova today, leaving the dog in the car. This truly is a tourist resort! I thought Papingo was a bit twee! It's literally as though Windermere or Ambleside had been transported to Greece. Shop after shop sold local wooden crafts. I left one with a salad bowl and wooden salad servers. I have no idea why.

We also bought two huge smoked cheeses which are apparently good as saganaki.

Wednesday 17th April

After a day wondering around in the drizzle yesterday, we were ready for our room, the stove and the bed. However, as we went back into our building, a German girl stopped us and asked if we could help her. She had been expecting her three friends for a couple of hours and she was worried. They were on motorbikes and the weather was now truly awful. We agreed to give her a lift to see if we could find them, as they had set off from a place only about twenty kilometres away. As soon as we climbed out of the village, it became very obvious why her friends were missing. Visibility was less then five metres and it was snowing heavily. We crawled along the narrow road, spotting hairpin bends at the last moment and sliding on the road from time to time. When we eventually found them, one of the motorbikes had broken down. Some complete twat of a guy was trying to tow it! I couldn't believe it. He had actually persuaded the German guy to tie his bike to the car! Between us, we managed to convince the very cold and pissed off German that this was not a good idea, and to come with us back to Metsova and sort his bike out in the morning.

We got back to our room after midnight, extremely cold and tired. It had taken over an hour and a half of seriously concentrated driving to make the seven or eight kilometres return trip, followed by the other bike. I was asleep before my head hit the pillow.

Feeling very much the Good Samaritans, having rescued one dog and three Germans, we are setting off this morning for Kalambaka, and The Meteora.

Thursday 18th April

Yesterday, Spring sprang! We drove into blue (ish) skies and the best weather we'd seen for two weeks or more. The bigger monasteries were fairly busy, but as we had the dog in the car we decided to resist. However, the clichéd 'spectacular' does not do justice to the visual impact of The Meteora. Breath-taking, astounding, inconceivable, spiritually stupefying. The mountains are weird indeed, towering high above the plain with sheer drops all around, and filled with smooth holes like some kind of monstrous Swiss cheese.

Some of the monasteries seem to defy gravity (and common-sense) as they hang there, tenaciously gripping on to the mountainsides.

When we left, having lost and then re-found the dog, we drove to Ipati, to try to find somewhere to stay. It was still closed up, not yet ready for the season. The only place we found was positively shabby. Although it was already late, we decided to drive straight back to Athens, and arrived in the early hours of the morning.

This morning, back home, we were woken early by the dog scratching to go outside. Oh, the joys of pet ownership! She scratches enthusiastically to come back inside, too. We also discovered the video we had forgotten to take back, and a fairly trite phone message concerning the same. That should cost a small fortune.

We now have to go shopping, dog food amongst other things, return the video and clean the car of dog hairs etc., before it is picked up tomorrow morning.

Friday 19th April

Woke late again. Frolicked around in bed with no particular urgency to get up.

Fed dog proper food, for which she seemed grateful, in a doggy kind of way. She seems to be putting on weight. She's very scared of everything though, especially sudden movements and loud voices. She's definitely been mistreated. We are calling her Pofi, which comes from '*pinalia ofi*' meaning, roughly, a hungry look. We are a one-pet family again. The continuing absence of Kaltsoula has a permanent feel about it, and not in a bad way.

Saturday 20th April

The landlord came around today and is seriously pissed off about the dog. There is absolutely no way, he says, that we can keep it. He also gave a very derisory grunt at Pofi's name; drawing attention to the dog's Greek name had been my attempt to placate him. He's given us a week to get rid of her. Abigail says to ignore him and see if he seriously threatens to throw us out. I'm more tempted to move.

Sunday 21st April

We woke to truly glorious weather. In an effort to prolong the holiday and put off the fateful morrow, we took off today to go to Xalkida. We left the dog in the flat - she seems to like it there and only ever sleeps in any case. Another idyllic day in paradise. Again, I can't help but wonder if I deserve to be so happy. Abigail really is just about everything I want out of life, being with her justifies my existence. Being away from her can be physically painful. I know enough to understand that this cannot be healthy, and hence I question it nearly all the time. What would I do if she were to disappear tomorrow? I'd crumple up into nothingness, I'd fall into myself, and my world would stop. My shallow self tells me to forget such musings and get on with the business of enjoying it. My mature self, growing and learning, tells me to guard against such a tomorrow. My two selves confuse me: what happened to enjoying today and not worrying about tomorrow? Is that so foolish? In my heart I know it is, because in ignoring this annoying little voice in my head, I am courting disaster. I came to Greece knowing in my mind that I didn't want to depend on another person for my happiness. That was my job, no one else's. And now look at me! I positively need her. The thought of her maybe not being around one day scares me. It is beginning to grow in my head, beginning to be something I fear, beginning to be something which gets me down, when I have no other reason to be down. Why can I never just be happy?

Affirmation of self – II

> *Here, in what and where I am*
> *Reality, in all its forms does dwell*
> *Now, in what I do and feel, I am alive.*
> *Tomorrow, in fears and hopes, live ahead*
> *Ahead, with its twists and turns, is not fixed*
> *Life, the learning and the growing, is this*
> *Being, honestly and fairly, is my goal*
> *Growing, to be the best that I can be, is my aim*
> *Success, in whatever form it takes; contentment*
> *It is me, myself, my relationship with me*
> *That counts towards the person I want to be*
> *The future me*
> *Success, in the pleasing of another,*
> *Is failure in the growth of me*
> *If, in pleasing her, my 'me' is sacrificed.*

I'm not sure where that last bit comes from, why it has changed. Do I really spend so much time trying to please her? Yes, I guess I do. Having got her to come back here, I feel that I have a responsibility to keep her happy. My mature self knows that this is so much bullshit: she's a grown woman, making her own decisions. I am in no way responsible for them. That's all very well for my mature self to know and understand, it's my shallow and puerile self that has to deal with feeling guilty.

Monday 22nd April

School again. Kids pleased to see me, which is nice. Feel only a bit guilty that I am not pleased to see them. To be fair, I'm not displeased, just not positively effusive...

Tuesday 23rd April

We looked in the paper for other apartments. Abigail phoned a couple, but 'no pets' seems to be the norm. I like our place here, although perhaps somewhere we choose together might be better for Abigail, to make her feel more 'at home' rather than living at 'my' place. The old fear that she may pursue a place of her own resurfaces, stomach-churning; but, like any good coward, I say nothing about it and push it all to the back of my consciousness. She has interpreted this inner turmoil of mine as lack of interest in finding another place. I can't win.

Wednesday 24th April

In school they were already talking about opening the pool due to the good weather. Maybe even on Monday. Then I get to go swimming three times a week for forty minutes instead of working. My fitness regime ground to a halt over Easter. I wonder if I can achieve a flat stomach in four days? I think not. I shall try avoiding alcohol to see if that helps.

Have just done forty sit-ups as prelude to new, improved fitness regime! Forty sit-ups, twice a day. It'll only take about five minutes, how hard can that be?

Thursday 25th April

Not too hard so far. Managed forty sit-ups first thing this morning and again when I got in from work. Abigail is much amused by my attempts to lose my gut, which she says is fine anyway. She does nothing at all in the way of exercise, and is as thin as a rake. Sickening. And she eats so much chocolate!

Friday 26th April

It's official: the pool opens on Monday. It is summer! Well, nearly. Managed an extra set of sit-ups when I got in, to counteract the two beers I had while helping to set up the pool bar after school.

We are going out tonight with some of Abigail's Greek friends to a live music bar in Athens where there is a Gospel Jazz group on. Sounds interesting.

Saturday 27th April

Was interesting. A huge black woman with an amazing voice. We should go more often to this kind of stuff. Inspired, Abigail has promised to learn a piece of music on the cello for me, but won't tell me which one. She says it's classical and one of my favourites. I told her I didn't think I knew any pieces of classical music, let alone had a favourite. She told me to stop pretending to be a cultural Philistine and thus live up to my British stereotype. Ouch! Little does she realise, I'm not pretending.

Here are my achievements today:

I tidied away all our clothes from where they were strewn around the lounge from last night. (We got back rather late, and rather drunk.)

I washed Abigail's car while she was in town. She came back and didn't notice.

I fitfully 'studied' Greek for about forty minutes.

I managed to convince the landlord that we were looking for a home for the dog.

I started reading "The Tao of Pooh" in an effort to spiritually evolve.

I phoned Rachel, and caught up on her news, without feeling guilty for calling her. She consistently brings out the best in me.

I phoned Richard and arranged to go out on Tuesday evening.

Pretty impressive work for one day, I thought.

Sunday 28th April

Got really into the "Pooh" book today. Read it all while Abigail went out to see friends. Am supposed to be starting Reports (again!), but can't get into it. Surprise, surprise.

Monday 29th April

Woke. Ate. Worked. Ate. Worked some more. Ate. Watched TV. Drank large glass of whiskey. Failed dismally on sit-ups front. Going to bed. Life in the fast lane…

Tuesday 30th April

Wrangling with school again today over my salary. I came out to an exchange rate of 366 to the pound, we are now at 425. I was promised a UK protected salary, but paid in drachmas. The management of the school has conveniently forgotten this. I'm still not paying tax, so I guess it's not too bad, but I'm still pissed off. It's the principle. I have been duped out of money which was promised to me. I suppose at least I got paid today. I feel an extravagant purchase coming on.

I'm going out with Richard tonight, so maybe I'll just spend a fortune and get very drunk. We're starting the evening a new curry house in Kefalari. Should make a change from our standard evening diet of pizza. I have also resolved to stick to red wine and avoid beer on the assumption that it must be at least marginally better for me.

Wednesday 1st May

Took my first swimming lesson with the kids today. The pool is bloody freezing. It is, however, a sure-fire cure for a hang-over. There's no way I'm getting in it tomorrow though, not for anything less than a drowning child. Even then, it would depend on which child…

Thursday 2nd May

Watched the kids swim today. Basically sat and sunbathed for half an hour. Times like this remind me of what a good job I have.

Have been into Kifissia and bought some roses for Abigail and a bottle of Champagne.

Abigail seems really keen to move, all of a sudden. She's found four places in the paper, and wants to go looking at the weekend. Looking won't hurt, I suppose.

Friday 3rd May

Spent yesterday evening drinking Champagne and talking about ideal houses. Abigail was suitably impressed by her unexpected gifts. It gives me a real thrill inside to see her happy.

Saturday 4th May

A totally wasted day, driving around trying to find places which don't exist. Tried four *monokatikia* or little bungalows. One was imaginatively described in the paper as being somewhat larger than it was and having more by way of a roof then it actually had. Another was perfect, but without the aid of any heating system at all. We are still considering it as a possibility, as we could install a wood or petrol heater, but memories of this winter definitely sway us towards something centrally heated. The other two were not where they were supposed to be and so, after driving around for hours, we gave up. We phoned one guy four times in one village, and he kept directing us to the lane where "the dogs are barking". He was quite serious. That's just about every lane in Greece, so it wasn't surprising that we didn't manage to find it.

We now both feel tired and in need of a drink. Fortunately, both needs are relatively easily fulfilled.

Sunday 5th May

Did absolutely nothing today. Played the guitar just enough to convince myself that I am crap at it and should give up. Abigail got annoyed with my childish temper tantrum. Can't say I blame her. She took Pofi out for a walk while I sulked at home. I then spent a fruitless hour and a half watching out of the window in the hope of seeing her return.

> *Faith*
> *A gleam of light amidst a blurred darkness*
> *A glimmer of understanding amidst a thickening confusion*
> *A feint ray of hope amidst a swelling sea of despair*
> *Nervous courage pierces a wall of fear*
> *And against all odds, the living machine continues on.*
> *Faith - in what?*
> *In anything, it surpasses all else.*

Monday 6th May

Took the kids to a flower show in Kifissia this morning, which was a good skive. Managed not to lose anyone, which is always satisfying. Bought myself a small collection of cactuses (cacti?) and a Basil plant, because it smelt good.

Tuesday 7th May

Sports Day at school. Spent all day moving groups of children around and trying to keep parents from interfering. I am absolutely knackered and have the headache from Hell. Why is it that I'm doing this job again? Money and holidays. Think: money and holidays...

Thursday 16th May

An absence of a few days, on account of our having done absolutely nothing of note. I feel we have drifted into monotonous routine. Spent the weekend in almost a carbon-copy of the previous weekend. We did see one place we liked, but only from the outside as the guy who was supposed to meet us there just didn't show up. It seems to be an idyllic little bungalow set in about an acre of land. We got a bit carried away with ideas of planting vegetable gardens and keeping a goat! We phoned him the next day and he claimed that he had been there. We are supposed to go again next Saturday, but I'd like to go away for the weekend. Pofi would love it - the house, I mean.

I have been braving the elements at school and swimming with the kids. This is because it looks like I'm just sun-bathing when I just watch, which is apparently 'an unprofessional image' to show to visitors. Ho hum. I am to consider myself chastised. It still beats working for a living.

We are going to go away for the weekend. Richard has very obligingly offered to feed Pofi. Small amount of arm-twisting required and a fridge full of Amstel.

Friday 17th May

We are in Ermine, in the Peloponnesus. We found a gorgeous little apartment, with its own kitchen and a balcony overlooking the sea. Abigail is not well though, complaining of stomach cramps, and has gone to bed already. Not exactly the evening I had in mind. I'll have to be satisfied with a couple of cold Amstels and the warm sea breezes. It doesn't matter how good I make it sound, it's a poor substitute.

Sunday 19th May

On Saturday, Abigail seemed much better, judging from the early morning gymnastics! She even went down to the bakery and produced breakfast in bed, followed by further athletic exploits. Must be something in the air. Who's protesting?

We found a beautiful pebble beach at Saladi, and lay there in the sun. After a while, mildly erotic daydreams aroused, we looked for something more secluded. We found a perfect little beach, with not a soul for miles around. Making love on the shore, feeling the sun on my back and her body under mine, I found my Arcadia, my El Dorado, Nirvana, the true meaning of rapture: authentic bliss. Have I overstated that? If anything, understated. Strolling around naked on the beach, swimming, lying in the sun, making love again: we had found an idyll.

I'll never forget this day. It is simply without equal in my life. She makes me so happy.

Monday 20th May

And I shall never forget the trauma of leaving her in bed this morning. She fills my world and seems to be everything I could possibly want or need. To leave her, even for a few hours, to go and do something meaningless that any robot could do, seems woefully unfair. I just want to be with her, and for everything else to stop and leave us alone. Should I be worried about this?

Tuesday 21st May

The world didn't stop and leave us alone, so I had to go to work again today.

Wednesday 22nd May

Happiness
Defies equation
Becomes real
And from simplicity
Comes a complex reality
Needing no reason
Needing no substance
Happiness is a simple meal
A smile, a whisper
A thought second-guessed
A truth
From which we grow.
We create
We live
We love
We become
A personification of that which we seek.

Thursday 23rd May

My ritual of leaving Abigail behind in bed was made even harder this morning by her erstwhile attentions. In the end, I had to give in to my more natural impulses, phoned school to say I had some disastrous transport problem and set about being a bit late – an hour or so. Abigail didn't start today until eleven. She thinks that if going to work is such a monumental effort each day, I should pack it in and do something I like. She doesn't realise that leaving her to do anything else would be as hard! Doing something I like, right now, would involve keeping her at home all day too. This is not something I feel I can readily admit though, as it reveals the true shallowness of my nature. Such a revelation would not be helpful to my cause.

Friday 24th May

On the notice board in school today I saw a motorbike for sale. It had not occurred to me before that I needed another form of transport, but this seems cheap at two hundred and fifty thousand drachmas and I've always fancied one. It's a Honda CB 400 and is evidently not new, but I will see tomorrow morning when I go to look at it. Maybe this is the extravagant purchase I felt coming on!

Abigail is particularly keen on the idea, saying it would be great for the summer to go visiting a few of the islands. With only a month to go until the end of term, I suppose we should be thinking about what we're going to do. I'd like to spend the entire holiday with her, but I suspect she'll want to go back to Paris for a couple of weeks on her own. The thought of being away from her for so long fills me with foreboding - not just apprehension, but fear. The warning bells I haven't heard for a while now make themselves heard again. Only now the ring is more persistent and threatening. Am I in too deep? The question itself scares me, so I push it down into my depths again. Something is going to crack, and I'm worried it'll be me.

Saturday 25th May

I am sure that this could only have happened in Greece. Yesterday, for the first time, I considered getting a motorbike. Today I have bought one; it is sitting outside the flat now. I arrived to find that the bike belonged, four years ago, to an American doctor who lived here. He sold it for a song to another guy, who then sold it to this guy. Throughout both of those sales, nobody exchanged papers for the bike - it remained officially in the name of the American doctor. It has no tax disk for this year, and has not had one since 1993. The registration document is woefully out of date, and clearly has the wrong name on it. I questioned all of this, of course, to be told that none of it mattered. This guy told me that he'd been stopped by the police a couple of times, and each time had pretended to be a tourist who had borrowed his friend's bike. This, together with feigning to neither understand nor speak any Greek, seemed too convoluted a story for the police to want to get involved in, so they let him go… Apparently, all I have to do is stick to this story in the highly unlikely event that I am stopped. I asked him about maybe getting an up-to-date tax disk: he shrugged and said I could if I wanted, but he wouldn't bother. I asked him how to go about getting a bike licence, as I only had a UK driving licence. He again said he wouldn't bother - he'd been riding a bike in Greece for ten years without a license, and his UK driving licence had never once been questioned.

I told him that it was too expensive, considering it would never be legally mine and I couldn't sell it easily. He said that he never expected to get much for it, but to advertise it for less meant that nobody came even to see it because they thought that for the price, it must be shit. It's no beauty, but it runs smoothly, started first time and does one hundred and twenty km/h, which is already faster than I feel safe at. I ended up giving him a hundred and fifty thousand, and riding away the proud, if slightly dodgy and illegal, owner of a motorbike!

Abigail took one look, and was thoroughly unimpressed. She went for a spin with me and loved it though. She didn't raise an eyelid about the illegality of it: "This is Greece," she said, by way of explanation. She did more than raise an eyelid after our little spin, however, when I told her it was the first time I'd ridden anything bigger then a moped! It will take some getting used to, I think.

Sunday 26th May

Abigail has refused to come on the bike with me again until I have ridden around in traffic for a week. I suppose this was fair enough. I went up to Xalkida and back today, which was very tiring but exhilarating. Being there without her though, was fairly boring. Can't wait to see people's faces when I roll into school on this in the morning.

Went to visit Richard, just to show off. He wasn't in. Bastard.

Monday 27th May

Got told off this morning by my kids for riding a bike without a helmet. Nobody seems to wear one in the summer, so I'd figured it would be OK. Having thought about it though, I decided to get one. It's one thing being illegal, it's another thing compromising safety. Also, I am now insured! That proved very easy to arrange today - the insurance company didn't want to see any proof of ID, as it is the bike itself which is insured, and not the rider. It didn't seem to matter that I'd passed myself off as the American doctor whose name still, somewhat grandiosely, adorns the registration document.

After school I found a bike accessories shop and bought a helmet, a brake-disk lock, a pair of leather gloves and a luggage rack. I soon discovered that it was way too hot for the gloves, but I'll need them after the summer. It's also very hot wearing a helmet, but a small price to pay to avoid having the contents of my head sprayed onto the road, I guess.

I had a look at how to fit the luggage rack when I got home, but it looked very technical. I shall have to enlist help, DIY not being a strong suit of mine. Actually, not being a suit of mine.

Tuesday 28th May

It has now become very hot, with daily temperatures reaching the early thirties. It's amazing what a spell of good weather and a thoroughly spontaneous and possibly ill-considered purchase can do for the spirits! I keep patting the petrol tank affectionately and sitting on the bike where it is parked: veritable new toy syndrome.

Wednesday 29th May

A parent in school says she has an old leather jacket that no longer fits her husband which I can have for the bike. What can I say? She's bringing it in tomorrow. Colleagues suspect she has ulterior motives. Not my problem.

Thursday 30th May

We have begun seriously thinking about where to go for the summer. Abigail has one or two islands in mind which she still hasn't visited. I'd like to go to Amorgos and to Patmos. We spent this evening looking through the guidebooks and talking holidays. And yes, she does want to go to France on her own. And no, I don't know what I'm going to do.

Friday 31st May

I have been given what looks to me like a brand new black leather jacket. It's really good quality and can't have been worn more than a couple of times. She said it was only sitting in the wardrobe, and might as well go to a good home! Also invited me out for coffee 'any time' and gave me her mobile number. How come I never perceive this stuff coming?

Possibly made a slight tactical error yesterday evening in telling Abigail exactly how I felt about needing to be with her. We were having a fairly heavy heart-to-heart about feelings and being alone, following our holiday discussions. It seemed a good idea at the time, but she clearly does not like the intensity of being so needed. What surprised me was that she knew this already. How come other people are so bloody intuitive and I spend my life walking around in the dark? She feels I have put her on a pedestal, and worries about what will happen when she falls off. I denied it, telling her I had no such flawless images of her, but I know she's right. It's too much, this feeling I have - too strong - and something is going to give.

She tells me that I don't do enough for myself, like going out with friends and spending time on my own. Again my split personality fights over what is right: I know she's right, and that I should do more for me, but I feel I can't be away from her. When she goes out without me, I worry about her, who she's with, what she's doing. When I go out without her, I worry about her, who she's with, what she's doing. I don't like where this is going. I don't like this reaction I have to being away from her, but it's a real reaction, making me feel physically sick and I don't know how to stop it. She has gone out with friends tonight, as if to force me to face up to my demons. Thanks. A lot.

Saturday 1st June

She stayed out until three this morning, and I had to resort to alcohol to cope with the waiting. I have become a dependent slug, and I hate myself all over again. Why didn't I just go out myself and forget about her for an evening? Because I physically can't do anything else but wait for her to come back.

When did this happen?

Sunday 2nd June

Feeling thoroughly ashamed of my puerile emotional insecurity, I abandoned my day. Read and listened to music for hours. Abigail disappeared with the dog. Something has definitely changed here, and not in a good way. At times like this, thoughts return to Rachel. This is both immature and selfish. I'm also reminded of her very prophetic parting words, "I will be anything you want me to be, except someone else's understudy."

Drove my motorcycle directly into a parked car this morning as I released the clutch thinking it was in neutral. Fortunately no witnesses.

Friday 28th June

June has not been a good month. Felt generally indisposed towards writing.

School finished today. I felt more relief than anything else. This holiday is not a luxury; it is, for me, a necessity for my sanity. I feel tired in head and body. I feel the onset of depression clouding my view of everything. I feel lost to myself.

Abigail and I have been slowly drifting apart, the intensity and the ecstasy wearing thin. She's more and more exasperated with me for not doing enough for myself. I'm more and more frustrated with her for her wanting to do more for herself – her independence leaving me feeling undervalued, unwanted. I feel that going away together to the islands would either make or break us. I know right now that I'm trying too hard, and that, in my frantic attempts to keep what we have, or re-discover what we had, I know I am pushing her further away. I can't help myself; I just don't know what else to do.

Saturday 29th June

Rode the bike into Athens for the first time today. A good feeling of freedom and of possibilities which I have not felt for a long time. It is brilliant to feel that school is over and that I now have ten weeks ahead of me in which to recuperate.

I can't shake this interminable headache, which I know is an end-of-term stress thing. I'm supposed to be going to Richard's tonight to watch the European Cup Final (Germany vs. The Czech Republic). I can't find any enthusiasm or energy for it though. I am going to force myself to go, just so I feel I've done something today.

The 2nd Athens Rock Festival starts on Monday. Lou Reed, Elvis Costello and David Bowie, amongst others. Even this I feel I cannot face, although Abigail wants to go.

My diary has become depressing reading. Maybe that's why I stopped writing for a while. I can't seem to find anything positive to say.

Sunday 30th June

Didn't go to watch the football. Couldn't face the company. What is wrong with me? I hate feeling so depressed.

Spent two hours today fixing a luggage rack to the back of the bike. It is a universal fitting, designed for all types of bikes, except mine. I managed to get it on though, and to save some of the bits in the process. It feels slightly wobbly, but will definitely not come off. We're planning on going for three weeks, so we need room for two backpacks and a small rucksack. I will have to go and buy a collection of hooky, elastic things.

Tuesday 2nd July

We took the Golden Virginia from Piraeus at seven yesterday evening. A huge, foul smelling dinosaur - the ferry that is. Well, actually, Piraeus as well. The bike, once packed, has to be seen to be believed. Everything has a slight tendency to slide off to the left, and we had to stop from time to time to re-adjust it all. Having learnt that lesson, we'll be more thorough tomorrow when we re-pack. The trip was fun: it was the first time since I bought the bike that Abigail had come on it with me. What with all the luggage, it was a totally different bike to ride: much heavier and harder to handle. When we got to the boat, they wanted me to put the bike on its full stand. Could I lift it? Could I buggery. We ended up tying it with rope to the side of the parking bay, as I had seen another guy doing with a huge Africa Twin Honda. The trip to Samos took nearly ten hours. We slept fitfully on the deck, having found a corner which was at least semi-sheltered from the wind.

We sat in a little café which had just opened, and had what was laughingly advertised as 'English breakfast'. It actually consisted of two slices of toast, two pots of jam and a coffee. After a night of only half sleeping on the deck of the boat, however, it was welcome. We stopped on Samos simply to get the connecting boat to Patmos. We did, however, do a brief tour of the island on the bike, stopping for lunch in a beautiful village called Manolates. It was really picture-postcard stuff, with a little *platia* and a range of blue and green wooden chairs and tables. There was no-one in sight at all: a woman appeared 'as if by magic', like the shop-keeper in "Mr. Benn"! We ate and dozed in the shade of the impressive brilliant-fuscia bougainvillaea.

We are now again at the port, drinking frappé in order to stay awake, waiting for the boat to take us the short distance to Patmos.

Tuesday 2nd July

We arrived at Patmos Town just as the light was receding into that perfect soft haze which manual 35mm cameras were invented for. We found countless little back-streets and some beautiful old houses. We spent a good three-quarters of an hour taking photos of church bells and picturesque blue and yellow doors and windows.

Before the light failed altogether we found a perfect little pebble beach at Lambi, on the North of the island. We have just unloaded the bare essentials from the bike - sleeping rolls and bags. Abigail is almost asleep already. I console myself with staring up at the stars and trying to find The Plough. There's no moon, but it's still light enough to write by. Every now and then, I see a moving light, hundreds of miles high, as a satellite passes overhead. No shooting stars yet...

Wednesday 3rd July

We were woken by the sun at seven this morning. Went to Skala for coffee and *tsouvrekia*, a kind of brioche bread, before moving on to tour around the island a little. We went to see the famous cave of John the 'Apocalypsi', where he was supposed to have received divine messages from the Holy Trinity. Unfortunately, this cave has been turned into a true shrine, in the Greek sense of the word: it drips with gold and icons and garish statues of the apostles. I, for one, found this very disappointing. There were, however, a lot of people who had clearly come to Patmos in order to visit this cave, and who were quite impressed with it. Takes all sorts.

We stopped for coffee at Kambos and a little further on had a swim at Lavathi Beach. We are getting spoilt: the beach had about ten other people on it and it felt too crowded! Having swum, and not having a hotel room to retire to, we set about finding somewhere to shower. Immediately behind the beach was an empty summer house, the garden of which we managed to get into via an old stone wall. We showered with a hose-pipe under the shade of an olive tree.

Following a map which bore strikingly little resemblance to the island, we eventually found most of the beaches, but none turned out to be more suitable for sleeping than Lambi, so we drifted back here at about seven this evening.

Thursday 4th July

Swam this morning at six, just before the sunrise. Truly magical. A deserted beach, the gently warming sun and the warm salt water dripping off my naked body. Abigail found nothing sensual to act upon, however, and quietly but firmly pushed me away from her. Later, I swam again, Abigail preferring to stay on the beach and read.

Friday 5th July

Woke again very early, this time to the sound of goat bells. A small herd of them was making its way up the beach. They paid us absolutely no attention at all. Life at one with nature: this is a real boon.

We went into Skala again today, to find out about boats to Lipsi, which is supposedly very quiet and more characteristic of the islands as they were ten years ago. Turns out that there's a boat tomorrow evening.

Saturday 6th July, morning

Having decided yesterday to stay only one more night on Patmos, we set off determined to find a different place to sleep out rough. First thing we did was to manage to run out of petrol, which caused mild panic, until we rounded the bend on foot to find we were only a couple of hundred yards from one of the only two petrol stations on the island! Pretty damned lucky really.

We found a beach at Meloi and basically stayed there most of the day. Sand, sea and sun - what else could you want?

On the map, there was a little church called Panagia Geranou - churches often having little secluded courtyards, we thought we'd have a look...

There was a steep narrow dirt path up to the chapel, and I thought it would be a good idea to take the bike up it, rather than unpack everything and carry it up.... Fairly predictable results - the bike now has a bent foot rest and I have a nasty looking (and feeling) burn on my left leg. So much for my souvenirs of Patmos.

We started off on the flat roof of the chapel, having watched a spectacular sunset. During the night we had to abandon it and retire to the court-yard because of the wind. We must have moved to every corner of that court-yard, trying to find somewhere sheltered, without much luck. I don't think either of us slept more than an hour at a time and this morning I ache as though I've run a marathon - or as I imagine I would, never having actually run a marathon.

Evening - We are now on Lipsi, and have just checked into a room. A large bed, sheets, running hot water! The island looks beautiful.

Sunday 7th July

I think it must be about midday. Abigail is showering. We're just getting up. I feel as though I've slept for a week.

I feel there is a gulf between us now. It's in little things, conversational contradictions and moodiness. We don't converse well anymore - not as we used to anyway. I know it's normal for the bloom of romance to fade, but I feel that something is going more seriously awry. She pushes me away every chance she gets. I look at her sometimes and ask myself if all of this could possibly be transitory for her? Is she on her way elsewhere? I wonder what this has all been about. Either she doesn't really understand, or believe, how I feel about her, or she doesn't care, or she does know and does care, but is so destroyed by her past that she has to treat me as the malignant. At times, I feel barely tolerated, at others patronised - I'm beginning to feel that only rarely do I feel loved, and even rarer still do I feel wanted. I hate myself for not having the guts to just throw all this out for discussion, to give her an ultimatum about us. I know I'm too scared about what she'd say. I know too, that I'm delving into resources of strength and patience I didn't know I had, to see what can develop here.

I know I'm at a cross-road in my life. I feel I don't have the strength or the courage to make decisions for myself. I am tired of everything being a fight. She's everything I ever wanted, and I do love her - but where did the 'happily ever after' get to?

Why is everything so bloody serious? I used to have fun!

Monday 8th July

A second night's sleep in a bed. We had a little tour of Lipsi; it doesn't take more than an hour. We found a magnificent beach at Platia Gialo. It was a few kilometres along a really bad dirt road: great fun on the bike. The white sand stretched for a hundred metres and the sea was a beautiful, clear azure. There were three resident ducks and a donkey, all of which roamed up and down the beach cadging food off any likely donor. The beach being so difficult to get to, it was superbly quiet and calm. We spent the entire day in and out of the water, leaving only when we had to, knowing that the roads would be treacherous in the dark.

Tuesday 9th July

With such a beach within our reach, why go anywhere else? Abigail is completely lost in her own thoughts, as, I guess, am I. There seems to be no easy way to talk.

We had an ouzo at the only *kafenio* or little café on the harbour in Lipsi Town. Even after only a couple of days, familiar faces begin to appear, with conspiratorial smiles and nods. It's as though we all know we've found a kind of paradise, and feel school-boyishly guilty about being here.

Wednesday 10th July

Despite the apparent perfection of this little isle, we're off tonight in search of sponges! We're going to Kalymnos, famous of old for its sponges and sponge divers. We'll make the most of our splendid beach for now...

The ferry boat to Kalymnos – *"Nissos Kalymnos"* - is taking its time to get there! Abigail is sleeping. I find myself looking at her and wondering, 'What is it about this woman that captivates me so?' Sometimes, I feel I know for sure that it has something to do with inevitability, with fate, with past lives. When she sleeps, I feel at peace with her. So, am I in love with her, or with my false image of her?

Thursday 11th July

We arrived early this morning. After Lipsi, Kalymnos Town was horrible to see! It was like being back in Athens. We found a guy who had rooms, and followed his fruit truck for what seemed like miles to Panormos.

The whole place reverberates with the noise of cars and bikes; there's even an airport. I don't think we'll be staying here for long.

Friday 12th July

We tried to get a boat to Astypalea today. We missed the last one by about ten minutes and, Sod's Law, there isn't another until tomorrow. Abigail's very upset about this, but I figure we'll just have to make the most of it. We have come around the island to Bathi, via a spectacularly windy coastal road. It's a little valley of fertility amidst the grey/brown rock of the rest of the island, and in that respect, quite picturesque. We have found a beautiful room overlooking a quaint fishing harbour.

Saturday 13th July

Astypalea. We have found something more to our liking! The town itself, the port, is very typical with white buildings and tavernas. We have a huge room, in which we have spent all of today, talking, and talking, and talking.

She takes my silences as a lack of interest in her and a lack of passion for life in general. And to think, my silences are filled with inexpressible anxieties about our future, ones for which I lack the courage to confront out of a innate fear of rejection. She can't understand how I can be happier doing something she wants to do, and so be with her, than to do something I want to do, but be on my own. She finds it annoying that I will readily sacrifice something I want to do, so that we can do something else together. She cannot stand being put first in things, somehow feeling undeserving of this, feeling pressured into being the 'good' person I seem to think she is. And in that, I again sense some dark lurking secret which she is still not ready to share. To solve our problems then, do I have to be less attentive, less caring, more selfish? This seems to be what she's asking of me.

She thinks I am on some kind of saviour mission, trying to find out what's wrong and to fix it. She says, mysteriously enough, that I'm the last person who can 'fix' her, and that I shouldn't be trying. All I know is that I met someone who intrigued me; someone who, I knew, was suffering inside. It was clear to me that she had a very poor image of herself, and I tried to help her to see the incredible person I saw when I looked at her.

I discovered that the guy she had been living with was a German she'd met out here a few years ago. To keep her, he'd used emotional blackmail of one sort and another, often threatening to kill himself and finally, in July last year, he actually attempted to do so. Leaving him was a huge decision, ridden with fear and guilt. She says she sees me wanting to be with her all the time and fears that I will become just as obsessive about her. Do I fear that too? A question I choose not to ask out loud.

We talked about living together, about how she had said, when she came back to Greece, that she wanted to find somewhere of her own. I'm sceptical about this type of arrangement, although possibly mainly from an insecure and jealous viewpoint. A woman living on her own, to the outside world, is pretty much a single woman, and therefore, fair game. Particularly in Greece. This is a very chauvinistic and sexist objection, I realise. I can see that there would be some advantages to living separately, but for the moment all I feel is the fear that this is the first step of a break-up. We reached no conclusions though.

She insists that I have to find more of a life for myself outside our relationship. She cannot handle the pressure of being the centre of my world; this is, I suppose, fair enough. I hadn't realised I'd become so involved in her, so lost to myself, and that I had strayed so far from the path I had intended to follow when I first came out to Greece. Actually, I had realised it. Just hadn't completely admitted it to myself.

Sunday 14th July

Feeling rather maudlin, we went into the town to eat last night. We were eating at a taverna called *"Georgio's"* and kept noticing that people were really dressed up: rare indeed for an island. It turned out that there was a wedding at the little church in the town, and we watched as people paraded through the street. The groom and his entourage had to go to the house of the bride and, after suitable serenading and leaving of presents, take her with them back to the church. We waited, and 'people-watched' while the service went on. The Greeks are amazing: they get all dressed up, and go to the church, only to stand around outside, talking and smoking. Most of them must have missed the service entirely. It was awful for the bride and groom, because by the time they came out of the church, most of the guests had drifted off, presumably to wherever they were having the 'do'. There was a three-man 'orchestra' - violin, guitar and *bouzouki* - to lead them away. We listened to the celebrations from our chaste bed (they were in a hotel not twenty metres from us) until well into the dawn.

Our day began late, trying to catch up on lost sleep. I went down to the beach on my own, Abigail chose to lock herself away in the room for the day. Supposedly to sleep.

Monday 15th July

A quiet day, beaching together. Together in this world, miles apart emotionally and spiritually. I think we've both had enough of this holiday.

Tuesday 16th July

We are going back to Athens tomorrow, as this is basically no fun any more. In fact, it's been pretty lonely for the last week. Inside me, a child is stamping his feet and yelling, "This isn't fair!" I just want to be happy! Why is that so bloody difficult?

Wednesday 17th July

And so, Pireaus and Athens achieved. I don't want to be here. School, teaching in general, Greece even. I no longer want to be here. I have nowhere else to go though. Is this the ending I anticipated? It is an ending. This is not what I wanted from this life! I thought this time I'd do more for me, do more positively in general. But I've fallen again into the traps I unwittingly set for myself. My guardian angel must be very disappointed in me. It seems that it is not the number of lives, but the quality of each, that is important. My quality is lacking. Last time around, I thought I'd learnt this.

> *Unattainable goals*
> *Unattainable dreams*
> *Desolation awaits us all.*

Thursday 18th July

There is someone
In my head
-Not me
Someone pulls me down
Casts a cloud
-Not me
Someone drains me
Of myself
-Not me
Someone tramples
My enthusiasms
At their birth
Strangles my desires
Mercilessly
Before they evolve
There is someone
In my head
-Not me

Friday 19th July

I have spent today on the phone, trying to get a last minute flight to England. It's not that I particularly want to go there, but I have to get away. My obsession with Abigail is going to destroy us if I stay for much longer. I need to be where she is not. She does seem concerned that I'm taking off so quickly, but not so concerned that she's going to try to stop me. Maybe that's what I sub-consciously wanted.

Empty spaces
A numbness creeping
Enthusiasm sinks
Glasses fill
Emptying again
Numbness creeping
Answers elude
Questions fail
Glasses fill
Empty spaces
Empty still
Empty glasses
Music flickers to life

Pre-set moods
Empty emotions
Fill unfillable voids
Indefinable spaces
Nothingness reigns
Empty glasses
Empty bottles
Empty lives.

Saturday 20th July

Forgotten dreams
An imagined world
Comes apart at the seams
Abandoned hopes
Reality beckons
Different boats
A future wide open
In this fragile sphere
Nothing spoken
Empty spaces
An empty chair
Familiar but drifting faces
Union offers love
Sweet but barbed is the hand
That fits that glove
Solitude seeks itself
An answer awakens
Spiritual health.

I am at the airport in Athens. I have no idea what I'm doing, or why I'm going, or what I hope to achieve. My brain doesn't work, my body feels it is on auto-pilot. I have made no plans beyond landing at Gatwick. I have no idea where I'm going to go.·

... Head pounding, blood rushing as the uncomprehending face reality's mirror image in that of their own, losing their tenuously gripped new-found strength and assertions of individuality, of knowing aliveness, oneness, to be saddled with awareness of desperate, unbending, unyielding loneliness, pointless and taunting 'what ifs?' and 'if onlys' scraping as at their open wounds, but the blood is no longer running out; it's running out...

Tuesday 23rd July

Cornwall, England...

> *In search of an inner peace*
> *of meaning in me*
> *for being me.*
> *In search of a little space*
> *room for me*
> *to be me.*
> *In search of a new way*
> *to pass these days*
> *with more honesty.*
> *In search of a better road*
> *to enjoy travelling on*
> *to enjoy being.*
> *In search of a new reality*
> *a brighter truth*
> *and a clearer vision.*

At least I have had the decency not to run to Rachel. I couldn't face using her that way, though she would, I am sure, have welcomed me with open arms. I'm beginning to realise that I love her too much to treat her so badly. I think she knows this. Maybe I should call her and tell her this.

I am going to call her to tell her this.

Part Three

the omega

Wednesday 1st January

An ode to life
The moon in its illuminating lunacy
Is but a visitor to the vastness of its vacuum
The sun in its breath-giving glory
Is only a flicker of light in its infinite darkness
The swirling masses of beings that are its planets
Are but corpuscles in its veins
And its inexplicable, receding depths
Are romantic myths in the making.
But me? I am its heart
Its soul, its understanding and its fate
Personified
And for me,
All of this continues on
To learn, to love and to hope

The proverbial and ubiquitous new page, fresh start, new leaf, new beginning. My emotional roller-coaster year is finally over. Here comes another year, promising anew… Maybe.

The trick, however, is not to expect things to be better, not to believe in the false promise of the new year, not to invest my hopes in the arbitrary turn of a calendar page, not to live in optimistic dreams of a better tomorrow, but to remember my innate but sometimes failing belief in the 'now' and the 'is', not the 'maybes' and the 'ifs'.

We spent last night in Sindagma Square in the centre of Athens, beneath a giant Christmas tree made solely from electric lights, watching a glorious firework display. A Technicolor marvel to welcome in the New Year.

Snatched moments of true happiness. This Christmas, alone with one another, has been truly beautiful. Swapping traditions from our childhoods: she'd never had a sack from Father Christmas at the bottom of the bed in the morning or heard pretend sleigh bells in the night; I'd never been to a midnight mass or been carol singing. Despite the traumas of last year, I feel confident about us.

Thursday 2nd January

We have three days until the dread return to school. I have really enjoyed this holiday, not travelling, save between our two houses, and being free to relax and do nothing. We've cooked loads, including the Christmas cake that I started the day that Abigail moved out back in September. I think that it was purely to give myself something constructive to do instead of dwelling on my certainty that this was a prelude to her finishing with me. It wasn't, as it turned out; well, not immediately. Although I couldn't have seen it at the time, it has given us the space from each other and the time to ourselves which we desperately needed to survive as a couple.

She took the little house we had earlier seen together. I thought that it was a bad sign that it was still available, but actually it's a brilliant place. It's reasonably priced, has a huge garden, which the dog loves, and is idyllically 'villagified' and calm. When she moved out, we were getting on so badly that actually for the first few days - being busy with cooking, cleaning and re-arranging furniture - I almost enjoyed her absence. I genuinely missed the dog, though somewhat insincerely used this as my principal reason for visiting her nearly every day. I think she probably knew this.

On Christmas morning, the vegetables steaming away and the nut roast roasting, we sat outside in her garden, drinking sherry. It was twenty-one degrees and the sky was a brilliant blue. I once thought Christmas in the warm would somehow 'feel' wrong. I think that this is a myth we perpetuate in England because we know it is always going to be bloody cold and miserable at Christmas! Based on my Australian and Greek Christmas experiences, give me Christmas in the sunshine any year.

Friday 3rd January

We have now been back together for six weeks and three days: hardly a breakthrough. As a celebration, however, we are going into Athens tonight in search of a vegetarian restaurant I saw listed in one of the city guides. It's kind of a kick in the teeth for traditional concepts of counting the days, weeks and years that we have been together. Since breaking up was so totally inconceivable to me, I never really believed it at the time. In fact, we saw each other almost every day during those two months, and got on better than we had for ages. So I am resolved now not to think in terms of measuring the quantity and more in terms of celebrating the quality. I'm going to take her out to celebrate whenever I feel good, or whenever I feel she needs it, not for chance dates of the year, when maybe celebrating is the last thing we feel like doing. Forcing yourself to have fun because you feel you ought to is ridiculous.

Saturday 4th January

The restaurant was called 'Paradise Found' and was the first really decent place I had been to since coming to Greece. OK, that's a bit unfair. Some of the tavernas have been exceptionally great, but the novelty soon wears off and the restrictive choices soon become irritating. Here was a restaurant which served excellent red wine, in proper wine glasses, and had a huge range of starters, side dishes and main courses, plus, to Abigail's delight, desserts. A storming success, I must say; certainly somewhere we'll re-visit.

We got slightly carried away with the very good house wine, and certainly had too much to drive safely. This is a bizarre thing about living in this country. When I lived in England, I would be very sanctimonious about drinking and driving. It is simply something you shouldn't do, therefore you don't. Full-stop. End of conversation. And for a while here, I still wouldn't countenance driving with even one drink inside me. But it's like the seat-belt thing: nobody wears them. You get lax because you know you don't have to wear it, and soon you lose the habit. I know it's stupid. I used to think that legislating for that kind of stuff was overtly right wing - how can you dictate to adults about their own safety? It's my choice, surely? I know there are arguments about costs to the NHS for road accidents etc., and I guess having to put on a seat-belt is a tiny imposition. Anyway, here too you are supposed to too, by law, but it's totally un-enforced. (I once got into the front seat of a taxi, wearing a white shirt and a tie, and put on the seat-belt. When I got out, I had a huge stripe of dust across my chest: clearly the bloody thing had never been used before.) So, now I never wear one, much to the disgust of friends back home, who have to constantly remind me of the huge fine which they will have to pay if I don't put it on. The same thing has happened with having a drink and then driving. Everybody does it. Crap excuse, I know. Somebody once told me that it was safer to be drunk when driving through Athens at two in the morning on a Friday or Saturday, since everyone else was. At least that way you wouldn't be so scared by their crazed antics. It's something else which the police simply do not enforce: you can clearly see drunk driving in evidence in the late evenings, and I've never seen or heard of a breath-test being administered here. So, after several glasses of wine and a very brief discussion about whether we should leave the car and get a taxi, we decided to drive home.

The fact that we arrived in one piece does not justify our decision, and actually I feel quite guilty about it in the cold light of day. It is not something I want to do again. The seat-belt analogy doesn't really hold, I guess, since the potential to kill someone else isn't involved.

This is all part of the process which one colleague described to me as 'Greekification', or 'going native'. She told me that I had to promise myself to get out after my three year contract, or I'd be unable to return to 'civilised' society. I thought the implication was a bit rich, since we live in the recognised birthplace of civilisation, but I do get the point. I have already felt an uneasy restrictiveness when returning to the UK: the idea of not being allowed to do things doesn't sit well with the growing acceptance of a Greek way of life, where not being allowed simply doesn't enter into the equation. Not being allowed, actually, is often part of the charm of doing something!

Having stayed at Abigail's place last night, I came back home this afternoon. I have a term's planning to do, but realistically know that I shan't even pick it up until halfway through next week. It's due on Monday, but it can wait. Greekification? I satisfy myself with ironing a couple of shirts, doing the accumulated washing up, checking the ever-leaking oil of the motorbike and removing the remaining traces of Christmas. I know it's not the twelfth night yet, but there's nothing sadder than returning from the cold normality of teaching only to find that it's still Christmas when you get home.

Sunday 5th January

One of the disadvantages of living apart is that our phone bills are enormous, though not quite as enormous as mine was when I was attempting to persuade Abigail to come back from France this time last year. Actually, there were quite a few calls to Australia in that particular bill, I seem to recall. Which reminds me that I must write to Rachel soon. I did send a Christmas card promising news in the New Year.

Last night I phoned Abigail to say goodnight and we hung up almost two hours later. I sometimes think we have better conversations this way. This morning, I went out early to the bakery, bought two croissants and two *stafithes* (literally: with raisins - a swirly kind of cakey thing, like a Danish pastry, but not quite as sweet) and surprised her with breakfast in bed.

We spent the day enjoying the garden in the unseasonably good weather. We found a roll of chicken wire and some stakes stashed in the shed and I thought it would be a good idea to make a chicken run and keep chickens up there. Abigail needs convincing though. I think it would be fun.

Back at my place tonight. I actually quite enjoy all this to-ing and fro-ing. I'm turning in early before the odious return to school.

Monday 6th January

Odious was the right word! There is no spirit, no 'feel' to the place at all. Maybe my New Year's resolution should be to get out. It was good to see the kids, of course, and to hear all their excited tales of Christmas.

But the moaning has already begun, the despondency of those trapped in a job they're unhappy with, the petty politics surfacing even now. I am not going to be doing this when I'm fifty. I'm going to be thirty this year - it's time to decide what I want to do when I grow up.

Tuesday 7th January

I am hearing
My cries from within.
Beginning to understand
The power I have to grow.
Beginning to see
That in me there exists my saviour.

101

Beginning to believe
That I can be self-sufficient
Beginning to have faith
In the me I am at my best.
Beginning to feel compassion
For the me I am at my worst.
I am hearing
My cries from within

Wednesday 8th January

The second day in a row of continual rain. Not happy motor-biking weather. I nearly came off it for the first time today, veering madly to one side to avoid a car coming from nowhere to join the main road. The back wheel skidded and by some utter fluke, I missed a parked car by jumping onto the pavement. Somehow I didn't get a flat tyre in the process. And the bastard just drove off as though nothing had happened! I arrived in school hopelessly wet through and shaking like a leaf. Tried to phone Abigail, just to hear a friendly voice, but she'd already left for work.

An interminable day in school, followed by hassle with the bike. I'd borrowed a set of very fashionable bright yellow waterproofs for my return, only to discover that the bloody thing wouldn't start. It does this sometimes when it's very wet. I spent fifteen minutes running it up and down the car-park, trying to jump start it. Eventually it spluttered reluctantly to life. I got home by five-thirty, had a hot shower and slept for an hour.

Abigail came around and cooked a *spanakopita*, or a spinach and feta cheese pie, and we had a quiet night in with a bottle of Hungarian Cabernet Sauvignon and a mediocre video. She wouldn't be persuaded to stay the night though, which was disappointing, especially since I thought I was at my most persuasive! Promised she'd stay tomorrow.

Thursday 9th January

Same crap with the bike this morning, but as I live on a hill, less of a problem than when at school. I was asked for my planning today, oops... Buggered if I'm doing it tonight. Abigail's due round in an hour, and I'm cooking pizza. Cooking: as in flour and margarine and fresh tomatoes and real mozzarella. I'm getting quite good at this stuff. I find it quite therapeutic to knead the dough. I must try making bread one day.

102

Friday 10th January

POET'S day! Piss Off Early, Tomorrow's Saturday. It's been a very long week. When it rains, the younger kids can't go out - God forbid they should get a bit wet! - so they are stuck inside all day and by early afternoon are usually climbing the walls. Spent lunchtime doing my planning in the library - it's very short, verging on woefully inadequate. Right now, I'd love to be told it was unacceptable, to be given the excuse to blow up at someone, to walk out of the job without having to first worry about the implications...

Saturday 11th January

Had a night out with Richard last night for the first time in months. It followed a predictable pattern. Talked for a long time about Rachel. Richard's of the opinion that there is possibly no greater person on Earth and I should high tail it off to wherever the hell she is. Not helpful. Somewhat stupidly, I decided I was OK to ride my motorbike home, since it's only about half a mile...

I remember getting back to Richard's house, I remember telling him I was okay to ride the bike and I remember a jeep blaring its horn and chasing me. I took a side road, and he followed. When I eventually stopped, the guy jumped out and before I knew what had happened, he had taken the key from my ignition. He was yelling in Greek, and even I could tell he was more drunk than I was. Apparently, I'd clipped his wing mirror with mine, and both were broken. I managed to demand my keys back, in Greek, when his friend appeared in another car and tried to calm him down. Then, from nowhere, a police car arrived and I remember sitting on my bike, keys in hand, being dumbly aware that everyone else had gone. The raving guy had driven off, tyres squealing, and the police car disappeared in pursuit. Through a window of unnatural clarity, I noted that I was left with only a broken mirror to convince me that any of this had really happened...

When I got home, I was glad to be living on my own. I'd have hated to have to relate this story to Abigail. That's the last time I drive anything after more than one drink.

This seemingly simple episode has made me think. Something to do with mortality I guess. A good dose of philosophising never did anybody any harm. Actually, that's probably not true, but anyhow...Above all else, you need to know yourself, or one needs to know oneself. Each of us is the only person with whom he has to live out his life. You are the only person to whom you have to be true, to whom you really owe something. This becomes an extraordinarily scary thought. Within the microcosm of society in which I live, there is no great truth or import. I teach for the money they pay me and for the holidays which afford me the opportunities to get closer to myself. Increasingly, I am at odds with teaching: the philosophy is becoming so crass that I feel I can no longer ignore it. I feel I am prostituting myself, and for no greater purpose beyond security and fear of stepping out to do something different, something potentially worthwhile. Working just gets in the way of the truly important parts of my life - getting to know me, to understand and appreciate myself, and getting to know Abigail, and to find a way to love her without crushing the life out of her. I am almost thirty and I feel I am doing nothing meritorious, nothing meaningful, nothing I can believe in or take pride in.

Buddha once said, reportedly, "There is only one time when it is important to wake up. That time is now".

> *A thousand places to go,*
> *Worlds and people*
> *To know*
> *A thousand dreams to follow,*
> *Imaginations, fantasies*
> *Can only grow.*
> *Things to do, uncountable*
> *Books to write*
> *A career to go.*
> *A million things to learn*
> *About loving, about me;*
> *About loving me.*
> *Yet only one lifetime*
> *In which to do it?*
> *Surely a lie?*

Sunday 12th January

I managed to find a bike place open on Saturday afternoon and replaced the broken mirror. It's plastic, not metal and it's round, not oblong: I wonder if Abigail will notice?

Having spent the large part of Saturday nursing a hang-over (the first of the year, I might add). I eventually went up to Abigail's in time for an evening meal together. She was bothered that I hadn't come up earlier. It was good to be missed, and a suitably romantic evening ensued. We are also still in the throes of renewed sexual appetites, which I can't help being inanely happy about. I know there's more to a loving relationship than sex, but…

On a whim, we decided to go and buy some soil and large plant pots and to re-pot Abigail's collection of plants. We spent about four hours with cactuses, lemon trees, Benjamin trees and bougainvillaea. I haven't had such a good time simply 'being' for ages. I need to spend more time doing things and less time thinking about them.

> *Hands in earth*
> *Creating something*
> *Achieving something*
> *Out of a few hundred drachmae*
> *And some few hours work*
> *Of emptying and filling*
> *Life will spring forth*
> *Living and new*
> *What can be more glorious than this?*
> *Simplicity*
> *Touching nature*
> *Today I have felt truly happy.*

Monday 13th January

I'm making progress. Although it's still hard to leave her in the morning, it's no longer the end of the world. I am regaining a balance, levelling out and rejoining normality. I think my obsession is on the verge of leaving me. I know that this growth has been forced upon me by her moving out and finishing with me, but it is growth all the same. Our time apart has made our time together all the more sweet. Our separateness has accentuated our togetherness; less is more. The agonies of last summer almost seem worth it now. Almost.

Tuesday 14th January

Gentle bollocking from the boss for the state of my planning today. Managed, as usual, to blag my way out of it, claiming to have handed in my rough plans by mistake. Don't think she really believed me. Means I have to work tonight: Sod's Law particularly enjoying times like these, Abigail has just phoned to ask if I'd like to go over to hers for an early night. It's now 6pm. I don't get offers like this every day of the week. Of course I'd bloody well like to. Having explained my predicament, I find myself seriously questioning my priorities. She says she'll come down in two hours to tear me away from whatever I'm doing. Two hours is about half the time I need...

Wednesday 15th January

A long, hard day in work, after a long, hard night. Managed to avoid the boss all day and finish off my planning whilst palming-off my PE lesson, my break duty and story-time onto my class assistant. She's a star. I owe her big time. I'll be stuck with her wet playtime duties for the next two weeks!

For last night, it was worth it. I'm shallow and superficial, I know.

Thursday 16th January

It has now been raining, on and off, forever. It's cold and windy. This is Greece, for God's sake! The Mediterranean! It's criminal what they teach you in Geography these days.

Tuesday 21st January

Friday was quiet - watched "Husbands and Wives" which was great - very Woody Allen. On Saturday we went out to a party in Halandri. I found it pretty boring. My Greek is passable, if I'm asking for directions to a train station or I want to tell someone I'm from England and have been living in Greece for two years and such. Once conversations get beyond that fairly primitive stage, however, I'm reduced to the role of listener and of nodding sagely when in truth I have understood little more than a gist. After about an hour, my brain registers overload and switches itself off, like a cerebral screen-saver. Five hours is almost unbearable, and whiskey seems the only successful lubricant. I can't wait to get the hang of this language; I'm sick of feeling the outsider. Abigail says I always will, that it's a social and cultural isolation, not a linguistic one. I'd like to be sure for myself.

Got back home to her place at 4.15 am to the onset of torrential rain...

And it rained for 36 hours! Tumultuous, violent and incessant rain. Sunday we spent more or less in bed - it was dangerous to go anywhere. In the Peloponnese, cars were being washed away! Any excuse is a good excuse for a day in bed. Monday morning was another bike story - could not get the bastard started! I shouldn't have tried getting into work; even with my so-called water-proofs, I arrived like the proverbial drowned rat and very late to boot!

Today has been fine, though, and now I sit with a none-too-good glass of white wine, contemplating my navel. I'm on my 'Where am I going in life?' tack again. Morbidly introspective, that's what my dad called me on the phone the other day. He talks about introspection as though I have a choice. But I have seen the void, the chasms, the emptiness which exist in a bigger reality than this. The petty world in which we strive and suffer is an illusion. I have to break through the illusion, see past the appearance of reality, to find my higher self. I have to rise above the detail and emotion of the game I am in, in order to recognise it as a game, to have perspective. I am in control here; I can choose the direction and the plot...

> *The reality we see*
> *Derives from ourselves*
> *And in it we grow.*
> *A lover's touch*
> *Or a sunny day*
> *Clear the air.*
> *Our fears and our worries,*
> *Our insecurities,*
> *Become fatuous, trivial.*
> *A quarrel,*
> *Perceived insult or rejection,*
> *Darken our perception*
> *Nugatory concerns,*
> *Annoyances,*
> *Take on monstrous proportions.*
> *The secret of the game*
> *Involves knowing this*
> *And keeping perspective.*

Wednesday 22nd January

I actually thoroughly enjoyed today in school. I made significant progress with one child, I had a conversation worth having with a colleague (not actually as rare as I imply) and I left work, for the first time in months, if not in over a year, feeling I'd accomplished something. I wonder why this should happen now, all of a sudden?

I went straight up to Abigail's place, buying flowers en route, and cooked dinner. She came home ecstatically pleased to see me there, which was a completely unexpected bonus to my day. She had a truly lousy day, in terms of in-house politics, and was ready to quit on the spot over some technicality in her contract. It's not my place to advise her on what to do, but I know she's feeling trapped by her job. It offers her basic security, but it was only ever meant to be a stop-gap. My unexpected good day appropriately counter-balanced her uncommonly bad day; all in all, not a bad state of affairs. This is what loving and supporting relationships are all about. Isn't it?

Thursday 23rd January

In celebration of Thursday, we are going out to a taverna in Nea Erithrea tonight. It has been some time since I last had *saganaki* and *xorta*, so I'm actually quite looking forward to it. Humble pleasures. I amaze myself with my ability, only on the odd occasion, but more frequently than ever before, to simply be happy. It's not so hard (he says, optimistically).

Friday 24th January

Oh, the hectic frenzy of life in the fast lane. Work, followed by a well-earned siesta, followed by a meal cooked for me at Abigail's place, followed by a good film, "La Gloire de Mon Père", and retiring to bed with the woman you love. Who said, "Life's a bitch"?

Not from here it's not.

Saturday 25th January

It's been a while since we've been anywhere. The travelling between two houses seems to have been enough to keep us happy until now. Today, however, we decided to get well away from Athens and go North to Evia. We've felt the winter chill in Anixi and from the house we can see snow on Parnitha. Somehow, though, it doesn't seem real.

Well, this was real. Abigail took me to a place she knows in north Evia, where there is skiing most years. I know they go skiing in Arachova, but that seems very far from here. Evia is only an hour's drive away. We drove through the village of Prokopi and on to the mountains. Having parked the car and walked for about a kilometre, we found ourselves in virgin snow. It was like a scene from 'The Lion, The Witch and The Wardrobe'. We could have been in Narnia. The fir trees, the eerie silence, and the crisp, even snow: I kept looking over my shoulder, expecting the evil Snow Queen to come charging around a corner in her sleigh. There was an undefiled layer of snow in all directions around us; ours the only footprints to be seen. That's the beauty of this country: somewhere this picturesque in England would be full on a day like today. And yet here we were alone; here, we could have been the only people alive on the planet. Abigail didn't understand my rapture. She's become used to such things, her Greekification being far more advanced than mine. It didn't matter: I was lost in myself. Moments of pure pleasure, true happiness, living in my snow-pure 'now', enjoying just 'being'. Nothing compares…

Sunday 26th January

Abigail's car chose yesterday, whilst still in the mountains, to get a flat tyre. I was not impressed. She did at least have a serviceable spare. I thought I would never get the feeling back in my hands though. We shared a hot shower when we got back to my place. No lasting problem with the feeling in my hands.

Outside: rain, cold, wind.

Inside: central heating, soft music, red wine, flesh on flesh.

Not a bad way to spend a Sunday.

Monday 27th January

I resent the intrusion of work in my life. Do I say this every Monday?

Tuesday 28th January

I resent the intrusion of work in my life. Just so that I'm sure it's not only a Monday morning blues kind of thing. It can also be Tuesday morning blues kind of thing. Actually, it's more a general blues kind of thing; it's going to need sorting out properly one day. And one day fairly soon…

I am heading for major battles at work. Greece is slowly teaching me to get in touch with my anger! I have always been very British in this respect: not wanting confrontation, accepting things which I am very unhappy about. The money situation is still a mess and I'm getting close to breaking point with the petty bureaucrat who seems unable to sort it out. Not only am I being paid significantly less than I was originally promised, but in addition, the real value of my salary has plummeted with the changing fortunes of the drachma against the pound. And now, I'm told that my two-year tax break might only actually be valid for one year. They seriously think that if they've fucked up, I'm going to fork out to cover the mistake. Wrong! Even so, I don't feel able to go in and stamp and shout, even though it might make me feel better. If I can't get sufficiently angry enough about this to actually do something, what is going to piss me off enough to kick start that emotion?

I have always had a problem with anger. It's as though I'm afraid to let it out, in case it's too strong. The persistent problems with school are simmering volcanically. Dangerous.

> *What is anger,*
> *When my anger*
> *Re-directed at myself*
> *Self-destructs?*
> *Keep the lid on,*
> *Pressure-cooker;*
> *Keep the pressure on.*
> *I can't work the slow-release.*
> *Hold the lid down,*
> *For if anger escapes*
> *It will erupt,*
> *All-destroying.*
> *What is anger*
> *But a bastard child?*
> *I should really know better*
> *I should 'control'.*
> *Anger is a devil*
> *That takes me from myself,*
> *Leads me to places*
> *I don't want to go.*
> *Anger is a friend.*
> *The explosion that is coming*

Can clear the way
For understanding.
I'm not ready yet
To embrace this friend,
But I'm beginning to see
He may be on my side.

Some friend. I sometimes wonder about the sanity of my poetic ramblings.

Wednesday 29th January

The bike broke down for good in Kifissia today. And it wasn't even raining. Tried jump-starting it, but no-go. So I had to walk back to my place, which put me in a foul mood. Unfortunately Abigail bore the brunt of it when she was foolish enough to ask me why I'd left the bike behind. She left a few minutes ago, saying that I could come up to hers later, when and if I'd calmed down. So, maybe my anger is beginning to leak out after all. Just in the wrong places.

Just now it occurs to me: go up later to Abigail's place how exactly? Without the bike? Very clever. I'll have to phone a garage tomorrow, from school…

Thursday 30th January

The only good thing about today was that it didn't rain. After a thoroughly pedestrian day in school, I had to go and collect the bike and push it three kilometres to a garage, as no bastard would go and get it. A new battery and another electrical-looking part cost me close to a hundred quid.

Abigail says she wants an evening in on her own: again, very correctly gauging my mood. I get the distinct impression that she's pissed off that I didn't go up last night, although we did talk on the phone for over an hour. Actually, it's not at all like her to play stupid games of that nature, so perhaps she genuinely wants time to herself. I must stop attributing my motives to her actions. It only ever complicates things.

I'm going to retire to the couch with a bottle of retsina and see what dirge Greek TV has to offer on a Thursday evening.

Friday 31st January

Bike wouldn't start this morning. So much for the repairs.

Am going to surprise Abigail with a candlelit dinner for two tonight. I even bought Champagne on the way home today. It's just a shame that the flat doesn't have an open fire: that would be perfect…

Saturday 1st February

OK, so no open log fire, but otherwise, perfect.

Sunday 2nd February

And more of the same. Spent the day dining on cheese, fresh bread, red wine and each other. Is it any wonder I get the Monday morning blues so badly? Who needs the real world?

Monday 3rd February

It's turned really cold, all of a sudden. Yesterday was 18 degrees in the sunshine, today it's overcast and a miserable 9 degrees, which feels like zero on a motorbike. I wore two jackets today, as well as shirt, vest and fleece. I went up to Abigail's straight after work only to find her out. I waited for about an hour before getting bored and going home to find a note from her asking me to take Wednesday off school so that we can go somewhere. It's a surprise. She'll see me tomorrow evening.

Tuesday 4th February

Perfectly boring day in school, enlivened only by my attempts to convince people that I was feeling distinctly unwell. I never claimed to be dedicated.

Wednesday 5th February

Having phoned in sick, very convincingly, I thought, Abigail and I drove down to Cape Sounion, where a friend of hers has a summer house. Not being summer, it was empty, and she'd got the key. This is where she'd been on Monday evening. She'd planned an impeccable seduction! It must have hit a chord the other night when I said it was a shame about there being no open fire. There is an enormous fireplace, with logs piled high to one side and black metal tongs and a poker hanging from a hook on the wooden mantelpiece, and it was all laid ready to be lit. There was a huge futon in the living room, wine glasses and massage oil on the fireside table. As if on cue, once we'd lit the fire, it began to rain, the light drumming against the window pane accentuating the warmth and comfort within.

It became clear that this was not going to be a one day illness.

Friday 7th February

Returned to school to concerned queries about my health. Was I sure I was okay? Shouldn't I have stayed away until the weekend? Any decent human being would have felt guilty.

The secretary gave me a knowing look as she said that she'd tried to phone me "a couple of times", but "you must have been at the doctor's". She also added, rather mischievously, "I know you've got a good doctor." Abigail assured me that she didn't tell anyone and that her friend has no connection with the school at all. How come women can be so intuitive?

Abigail's going out with another friend tonight, an ex-colleague from the hospital, and I'm going to a taverna with a bunch of people from work. One of the teachers in the Secondary section has a birthday. I vowed never to do this stuff again, but as Abigail's out anyway, and Richard says he'll come too, I guess it'll be okay. I'm riding my push-bike down there so that I'll have no temptation to drive anything motorised back home!

Am back home. All in all not a bad night. There were about twenty of us, which is becoming too big a group for me nowadays. There was the standard taverna fare. Trudy showed up, which was something of a blast from the past. I'd heard, through Richard, that she'd gone back to Denmark. She seemed reasonably sane though, which was a relief. She was all over some guy she'd just met at a party a few days ago. He's in for a good night.

I was glad to leave them all behind and go for a quieter drink with Richard. We were both with our bikes, so we found a little bar neither of us had been to before, kind of halfway between our flats. He told me he had just split up with Renata. I realised that I hadn't seen her in nearly a year, and that this was only the second time I'd been out with Richard this year. I took the occasion to apologise profusely for my self-obsessed absences. We have vowed to do this more often – just the two of us, downloading and unwinding. As I seem to recall mentioning one before, he's a truly great guy. I suspect I drunkenly told him this.

I'm definitely relying too much on Abigail's company. Too much of a good thing…. But it is such a good thing.

It's 2.30am and I resisting the temptation to call Abigail:

(a) just because I love hearing her voice just before I go to sleep, and (b) to check that she's back home.

I'm not calling because:

(a) likely as not I'll wake her up and she'll be pissed off and (b) if she isn't back home, I don't want to know and to worry all night about what she's up to.

Saturday 8th February

Abigail came around last night, or rather this morning, at about half three. She'd clearly had a good night. She just crashed into bed and slept. This morning she's as lively as if she'd slept twelve hours and no sign of a hang-over. There's no justice in the world.

Sunday 9th February

Sat in Abigail's garden, again enjoying unexpected sunshine (the weather's nuts in this place). We began talking about how good it could be if we tidied it up a bit. I went so far as to suggest that a pond with fish would be good. Spent the afternoon digging said pond, three-quarters of a metre deep, two by four. Should have thought, before I started, of all the rain we've been having lately. By the time I'd finished I looked like I'd been mud-wrestling. Have to find some heavy-duty plastic to line it with - and some fish.

Monday 10th February

Rushed around like a lunatic after school today to find and install the plastic sheeting and to fill the pond with water before Abigail got home. By the time I'd done it, however, it was already dark and Abigail could see nothing under the moonless sky.

She'll have to wait until tomorrow. There are two resident terrapins and four goldfish which I haven't told her about. They were great fun to transport on a motorbike! We'll have to find some kind of weed and a

114

load of attractive-looking stones to go around the edge and hold the plastic in place. Didn't think of any of this when I started.

Tuesday 11th February

I got a phone call from Abigail at seven-thirty this morning. She'd found the fish.

Apparently, we are going to spend next weekend beautifying the pond. How domestic. Abigail says she feels sorry for the fish and terrapins, having nowhere to shelter or hide. Shelter or hide from what, I ask. From each other, she rejoins.

They're already in nearly eight cubic metres of water, as opposed to a fraction of that in the pet-shop tank. They should be bloody grateful. We are going in search of arty bits of wood and rock tomorrow. Pofi also gets a long walk out of it.

Life stops for two days now, as some idiot invented Parents' Evenings. Note the plural. Not only do I have to teach all day on Wednesday and Thursday, I also have to return to school each evening at six and probably get to stay there until gone ten. At least Friday is Valentine's Day: something to look forward to. Being the incurable romantic that I am, I've booked a table for two at a Mexican restaurant.

Saturday 15th February

Last night was actually fairly nondescript. The meal was good, but Abigail seemed far away and I was really tired from my full week in school. It's probably symptomatic of expecting too much from an evening, setting myself up for disappointment. Abigail couldn't be persuaded to enter into the spirit of the evening when we got back. We went straight to bed, to sleep off the margaritas.

This morning we went on our search for rocks and wood and found a lot. Abigail's car won't take it all in one go, so we'll probably end up doing a few trips. We'll probably go again tomorrow and take the dog out. We managed to make the pond look reasonable though, and I purloined some pond weed from school, so the guys all have somewhere to hide.

Sunday 16th February

What a weekend! Back and forth about six times, and all for a casually suggested pond! I hope the fish survive now. I'll be really pissed off if we come back after our half term holiday to find them all floating belly up…

Monday 17th February

Booked two tickets for a flight to Paris today. I've got an old college friend living and working in La Défense, and we're going to crash there. Apparently it's very cold there just now. That should please Abigail.

More trouble at work. Evidently, I upset a parent on Thursday evening by pointing out that her son was not going to be an Einstein. She took offence, apparently, and has made official complaints about my insensitivity. Why can't these people get a life? Who the Hell wants Einstein for a son anyway? What's wrong with a bit of plain-to-goodness-honesty? It's not as if I said, "I'm sorry madam, but your son is as thick as pig shit and there's nothing I can do about it." I didn't even accuse him of being 'not especially bright' or 'not destined for academia' (which is one of my favourites). I simply said he wasn't going to be an Einstein. Uppity bloody parents with nothing better to do but interfere in things they know nothing about. I wonder if she'd have been offended if we had been talking about PE and I'd said that little Benjy wasn't going to be a Lynford Christie? Stupid cow.

Tuesday 18th February

Unbelievable. Had 'an audience' with the Chair of Governors today over my 'alleged' unprofessionalism. He says he's right behind me, wants only to clear things up, he's sure it's nothing. So why is he involved? They have no idea what unprofessionalism is. I can do much better.

Richard came up with me to Abigail's place for dinner. It was nice. Why haven't we done that before?

Wednesday 19th February

Stupid cow with thick kid has withdrawn said kid from my class, apparently for fear that I might victimise him. I would have been bloody well tempted, too.

The Head has suddenly remembered my other 'upsetting parent' incident. She thinks I should go on a course "to explore ways of dealing with parents". I have plenty of ideas of my own - for this parent at any rate.

Abigail thinks this is funny. She's probably right.

Thursday 20th February

I came up with a winning stance today, much to the disgust of the boss. The child in question returned to my class, and I asked the mother if she had something to say to me, as she had made no complaint to my face on the actual Parents' Evening. When she said, "No", I told her I was prepared to forget her slur on my professionalism and let bygones be bygones. She went a very deep shade of red and disappeared. Two minutes later the Head appeared, irate, apparently under the impression that because she had told me not to talk to the mother, I wouldn't. That's her problem.

I refused to discuss the issue with her. She relented finally, saying it was probably a storm in a teacup and it would blow over by the time we all came back off holiday. She hopes. I couldn't give a fuck.

Friday 21st February

Tomorrow evening we are out of here. I'm ecstatic to be leaving. Tonight we're packing and drinking lots of wine. Bon Voyage and good riddance.

Sunday 2nd March

I'm sitting at the table outside at Abigail's place. It's Sunday evening. Four days ago, we could have died. Today, my ankle and wrist in casts, I am writing in a garden in the sunshine in Greece.

We borrowed my friend's car, Abigail driving as she's used to the strange gear system on the old Renault 4. Crossing a junction, green light luring us on, we were hit at over one hundred kph by a Range Rover coming through a red light from the opposite direction. Abigail remembers nothing. I remember seeing the car, inches from my window, and then rolling. I think we rolled over twice; the car certainly ended up far enough away from the impact point to have rolled twice. We exchanged looks as the car came to a halt, me from below, window smashed, with my ear to the road, her hanging above me by her seat-belt. 'You OK? Ouais, ouais. Et toi, ça va? Yeah, I'm fine.' We both jumped out as if unhurt. Unwisely, as it happens. I had broken three fingers, a wrist and fractured an ankle whilst Abigail had whiplash and concussion. We were, however, very much alive.

Thoughts on mortality again. Three things. As we left Abigail's place for the plane, I took my house keys with me. I didn't need them, but I felt an uncanny fear at the thought of leaving them behind. The key fob is an old Polish St. Christopher. I've had it with me always, without ever recognising any particular need. When we first arrived in Paris I had a really vivid dream. We were in a plane crash. The aeroplane plummeted from the sky, burying itself deep in the ground. But it felt like a fairground ride. There was an escalator to take people out of the smouldering wreckage. As the escalator rose, we could see that we were actually rising up out of a sewer. We walked away. Lastly, visiting the *Sacre Coeur*, I felt an impulse to light a candle - something I've never done before. Not to pray, not to ask anything, nor to seek anything, just to light a candle and enjoy the peace I felt within me. These things were not unconnected.

Then we hobble relatively unscathed from an accident which, judging from the state of the wreckage and the police report, should have killed us.

At that point, four days ago, did our two other selves die? Have they moved on, learning different things now? I wonder if they have regrets about leaving so soon. Are there yet other selves, still critical in a French hospital, learning yet other new things? I wonder what? And here we are, chosen to live out this life, this version of reality, this 'now'. I hope we can do it justice, I hope we can learn our lessons well. We are each becoming ourselves inevitably, and ourselves becoming better through knowing each other. We're alive, and I believe there is a reason for that. The reason might well be simple. It might well be us.

Monday 24th March

It snowed today! I woke up from a really disconcerting dream about having missed the alarm clock and not gone into school and having to explain myself over and over, only to see through the open shutter a good inch of snow lining the trees. I greeted this beautiful phenomenon with the poetic phrase, "Oh shit, it snowed!" Abigail then jumped out of bed to survey the scene, quickly opening the shutters of the bedroom doors before leaping back into the warmth of the duvet.

The bastards never told me about this weather before I came to Greece. I was sure that there must have been a clause in my non-existent contract about temperatures in the 30's, clear blue skies and a significant lack of snow. Winter has lasted now since the end of October and has, for the second year in a row, been notably wetter than my English expectations. And colder. How does it manage to be 6 or 7 degrees and feel colder than England did at 5 below?

The cause of my merriment, however, apart from my childlike fascination with snow, is that such weather led once in the past to the school being closed for the day as children travelling on the buses from the mountains surrounding Kifissia could not get in. Living now myself not far from such mountains, it seemed only right that such a puny excuse might also apply to me. I phoned the school secretary to ask if school was indeed closing. Alas no. However, I let her know that conditions were 'contrary to my attendance today'. I didn't phone the boss, coward that I am, on the pretext that I only have her mobile number and her husband told me only last week that they no longer had the mobile phone as it was routing even their local calls via Exeter. What else could I do?

So, after a furtive phone call to a colleague who also lives up this way, to check that she wasn't going to roll up for work declaring that all was hunky-dory road and weather-wise, I embarked upon an unexpected day off.

My first achievement was a mission of mercy. I fished the only terrapin I could find out of the pond and deposited him inside the house in a plastic bowl. He thereupon metamorphosed from ice-cube to living being. Very impressive. Can't find his friend though. I hope turtles have good self-preservation instincts. The fish have emigrated, I think.

Abigail has started a photography course which fills her Sunday afternoons/early evenings. The snow, of course, presented a photo-shoot opportunity. With her black and white, well planned and carefully executed landscapes, and my colour, point-and-snap pictures, we should have an interesting collection of the house, garden and environs under about 50cm of snow. It really did look inspiring, although I have to admit that I had a deprived childhood in terms of winter postcard scenes: picturesque though Cornwall is, it seldom snows there with much enthusiasm. The dog was most definitely not thrilled. It was her first sighting of snow since we found her, so maybe she has some unhappy memories of the mountains of Epirus. Walking along the rail-tracks in Agios Stefanos, and standing astride the coupling device between two stationary wagons, made me feel like a character from Dr. Zhivago. The old station house looked suitably ramshackle and exotic.

Having returned, ruddy-faced and numb-fingered, we set out on a car expedition to see how far we could get in the snow. Disappointingly, the focus of the snowfall does seem to have been Agios Stefanos itself. The snow petered out in all directions. In little over an hour, it had turned into a beautifully bright afternoon. Now there is barely any evidence of its having snowed at all, save for the constant dripping from the roof.

Tuesday 25th March

More snow! Hooray! Another day spent in the idle and smug satisfaction that is only this sweet when you know you're missing a day of work - and you're not ill! Furthermore, you're being paid.

Friday 28th March

Another exciting week '*à la Grecque*'. Generally exuberant about Wednesday being a National Holiday, only to be greeted by a day-long deluge of rain. This country is definitely no fun in the lousy weather. There is a marked lack of pavements - indeed, the only purpose served by pavements where they do exist is that of reserved growing space for trees and unlimited free parking for motorbikes. It does have to be seen to be believed. So, it is virtually impossible to move around on foot, as the rain quickly channels into mini torrents which overflow even the most protective boots. The collecting pools and, in many cases, lakes of water are then liberally sprayed by passing cars over anyone foolhardy enough to be walking along the roadside. I seem to remember commenting on this once before... We spent the day indoors - playing scrabble, of all things.

Things, sadly, had not improved by Thursday. Force 10 gales had swept the country during the night. The whole of Athens had ground to a halt by early morning. My bike predictably failed to start given its nocturnal diet of water, and I had to rouse Abigail from her slumber to ferry (an apt choice of word) me into work. We achieved this by way of a very long and wet stop at a garage to replace the virtually useless windscreen wipers we had picked up last year in a supermarket. So much for bargain hunting! We followed the course of the river that was once Kifissias Avenue and I arrived at work, very wet and very cold, to be told that we were closing. A fruitless three hours. So much for our selflessly noble efforts.

The continuing foul weather resulted in a predictable power-cut. We rejoiced in our wood burning stove, and I phoned Richard to gloat about it. He was shivering in his candle-lit house, taunted by a pile of sodden firewood outside.

So, on to this morning. A 7 a.m. wake up call from the boss telling me that we were closing again today! Once more it had snowed heavily during the night. We watched the news for a while in bed, electricity restored. Many areas of Athens were severely flooded again. They were showing 'now and then' pictures from 1994, and righteously demanding action from the national water company, which was supposed to have completed drainage works to prevent such a repetition of events.

There is snow over a metre deep in places where snow never normally settles. The roads can only be described with a Greek word: chaos. Only 10% of the Athens area has electricity, some areas have been cut off now for 40 hours. People are actually dying. We look at the TV screen, and are thankful that we still have a roof over our heads and no water swilling through the house. It seems, truly, to be a Third World country at times like this.

Sunday 13th April

So much for my daily diary, again. But I do have an excuse, of sorts. I have been ill. To catch up on a few things...

After the snow had abated, and the waters subsided, and I had my ankle and wrist casts finally removed, I might have expected to manage a complete week in work. 'Twas not to be. I was struck down by the nasty little flu bug which has been creeping its way relentlessly through school. I started to feel decidedly unwell on the Friday of the rains and stayed that way for five days, hovering around 38.5/39 degrees for most of the time. I slept a lot and watched a lot of crap TV. After a week at home, hovering on the verge of being just well enough to be bored, I was looking forward to going into school on the Monday. I should have known better.

I put in a request to teach another age group next year. I really can't stand the thought of spending another year teaching initial letter sounds and setting up 'Independent Play Areas' and 'Valuable Learning

Experiences' for four year olds. It was met with a significant lack of enthusiasm. If it isn't met with something radically different by June, I'm going to resign. I think I could make a living here by only doing private lessons, if I find enough of them. I have started doing some in any case, for a bit of extra money; I'm sure it's one possible way of surviving here. It would also give me time to write, if I ever get up the nerve to follow that route seriously.

Monday 14th April

Spring has sprung again. It seems to manage to do this almost literally overnight in this country. One minute, we're missing school because of snow and rain, the next we're taking the kids outside for PE in shorts and T-shirts. Bizarre.

It's almost Easter. We have been making various tentative plans. Tentative because Abigail's friend may be coming out from France, so we could have company for the first week of the holidays. We are tempted to do the hiring-a-car thing again, and see some more of Greece. .

Saturday 19th April

Abigail's friend, Monique, has arrived from France to stay for a week or so. Miraculously, she arrived on time. Miraculously, because she had booked an Olympic Airways flight, contrary to our advice, and was due to fly on one of their ubiquitous 24hr strike days. She luckily transferred to a British Midland plane in the nick of time. We are off to Ermioni in the Peloponnese for a few days.

Monday 21st April

Visited Hydra today with Abigail and Monique. I had read a little about the island and had seen the picture-postcard scenes of donkeys and cats, but nothing prepares you for the almost complete absence of engine-noise which pervades other islands, even at this time of year. We arrived by flying dolphin - a hideous invention, noisy and fast (like an aeroplane!) which seems, to me at least, to defeat the very purpose of visiting the slumbering isles. Beggars not being choosers, however, it seems apposite to travel this way rather than not at all.

Although already suffering signs of its summer invasion, Hydra remained modestly wrapped in her idyllic habit, deaf to the occasional fishing boat engine which was enough to remind one of the bikes and cars one couldn't hear. It made the quiet all the more enjoyable. Monique was very vocal in her appreciation of her surroundings - misinterpreting my quiet enjoyment as disapproval of some description. Why do some people need everything spelling out in words, precisely and loudly?

In a jewellery shop to the left of the port as you face the sea, I met an interesting and garrulous Australian woman who had lived on the island for 18 years. I asked her about the lack of cars and bikes and it seemed to be a subject she was happy to talk about. As she was telling me about how some people try to get vehicles on the island, and how general protest has always protected the peace and preserved the archaeologically-based ban, a heavy rumbling outside preceded the passage of a huge garbage truck, one of two on the island. This prompted the following story:

Twenty-five years ago, the island got its first motorised vehicle. It was an open-backed truck for collecting rubbish and hauling it out of sight to dump it elsewhere on this beautiful island. Just six years later, they acquired a second. This was a newer version, with a revolving drum which masticated the debris like some mythical monster of old.

Exactly one week after the acquiring of the second vehicle, on rounding a bend above the sea and waving to their friend Michalis who was fishing below, both drivers contrived to collide head-on with one another. The newer lorry plunged over the side of the road and into the sea, fortunately missing the boat and the presumably somewhat bemused Michalis. Apparently, villagers rushing to the scene, crossing themselves frantically, proclaimed, "Thank God Michalis didn't lose his fish!" Only in Greece.

The second story about the island was also a classic. She couldn't remember exactly when it took place, except that it happened immediately after New Democracy won a general election over PASOK. It had been a huge affair: microphones; decorations; bulletins; parties. On this particular morning, she was roused by the sound of arguing. No surprise here in Greece, but this had to be something fairly impressive to be enough to cause her to get up and open her shutters to have a look. She saw the town square full of tourists, with hardly a café seat to spare. In the midst of this, was a small moustachioed Greek, yelling at the top of his lungs at the two young men who were collecting rubbish and heaving it into the back of the rubbish truck.

Their argument persisted for a few minutes before the truck driver deigned to climb down from his cabin, hoisted his trousers and strolled to the rear of the truck to join the fray. Apparently the arguing continued for at least ten minutes, the revolving rubbish bin turning the whole time. Eventually the driver returned to his cabin, flicked a lever and the drum stopped rotating. He then casually sauntered around to the other side of the truck, to the accompanying yells of the small moustachioed Greek. He pulled at another lever which, unexpectedly, according to reports from surrounding tourists, regurgitated the entire contents of the truck on to the Square.

What had happened was that the New Democracy Party, having finished their celebrations, had neatly packed all of their trimmings, speakers, microphones, pamphlets, etc. in to ten large black plastic bags ready for collection later that day. The rest of the tale hardly needs telling. The unfortunate young lads collecting rubbish had enthusiastically dumped New Democracy's precious bags into the revolving rubbish drum. Ironically, had the arguing not taken place, most of the equipment could have been rescued before being thoroughly pulverised. As it was, the victorious New Democracy Party salvaged nothing and the small local paper had a field day the following morning reporting the joyous applause of the PASOK supporters during the entire episode.

These will remain my vivid memories of Hydra. We returned to Ermioni and the following day re-visited Spetses, which was also basking in the glory of the Easter sunshine but as yet lacking its tourist hordes.

Sunday 27th April

Easter Day, Sunday. Abigail had just taken Monique to the airport. It was about two in the afternoon as we set off in our rented Micra; hadn't we done this before? This time, we have the dog with us from the beginning. We drove north to Katerini. We didn't think much of it. It was interesting though, as all of the shop signs were in Russian as well as in Greek. We learned that Katerini is a very popular destination for tourists from the old Soviet bloc. It is also a large centre for the fur trade: almost every other shop was a fur shop. We drove through a criss-crossing of streets looking for a hotel room. We had the problem of the dog of course: we had to find a place where we could smuggle Pofi into the room unnoticed. I asked in the first hotel and was shown to a perfectly normal two-bedded room. The price was reasonable too. However, it would have been impossible to sneak Pofi into the room. We were not keen on the idea of leaving her alone in the car for the night.

Meanwhile Abigail had been looking at the map and had found a little road (well, more like a little sheep-track as it turned out) which led to a chapel. We found what looked as though it might be an ideal spot to put up the tent and camp for the night. It was 11pm by this time and very dark, so we weren't really able to tell. At this stage in the evening, after 10 hours in the car, we really didn't care too much. We fell asleep, the dog at our feet, to the distant sound of goat bells. That is what I love about this country: the freedom to do stuff like this.

Monday 28th April

We awoke with the sun. It was very bright and warm outside the tent. I pulled on my boxer shorts and strolled around barefoot. It was a beautiful feeling, the first real sun of the year on my body, my toes in the still dew-wet grass.

Easter Monday. Abigail was keen to make the most of this and to visit some sites of archaeological interest that feature ubiquitously on the map of this area. In Greece, visits to such sites are still free on Sundays and public holidays. We headed towards some ancient Macedonian tombs near the town of Vergina. We were in for an enormous surprise. Expecting a small and undeveloped site, we found the largest surviving Macedonian burial mound in the whole of Greece. What looked more like a deserted hill actually had a marble-columned entrance. Inside the mound was a museum. The museum featured many of the original artefacts in situ. There was subtle lighting, (well, actually it was quite dark) presumably as a means to further protect the delicate finds. There was much written information, amazingly in both Greek and English. Even in Athens, I had not visited such a well organised and interesting archaeological exhibition. Much impressed, we looked for the Palace which was the home of those whose last resting place the burial mound had been. The Palace however, although it did have a strong sense of history about it, was not a well-developed site, and looked as ruined and deserted as it probably had looked when first discovered. They also wouldn't let the dog in.

By about eleven in the morning our stomachs were telling us that it was time for breakfast. Searching for a good breakfast is always good sport in Greece, if usually frustrating. We drove to the city of Edessa. Desperate for a decent coffee and hoping against hope for a croissant, we stopped at the first café we saw. We ended up drinking a very poor 'filter' coffee and buying some equally disappointing croissants from a roadside kiosk. Leaving this sad scene behind us, we drove on and very soon turned off the main road to follow a sign that translated as "the high rock". Edessa being famous for its waterfalls, this seemed an appropriate stop. Where, of course, we found a café that would have provided the ideal breakfast!

We were intrigued by the old and crumbling houses we saw as we returned to the parked car. Walking a little way through the narrow streets led us to more and more of these oddly Tudor style houses. They were all in a bad state of repair, some clearly derelict, with only one or two showing signs of recent renovation. A little further on we found a delightful 'City' centre with parkland and rivers. We followed the sound of crashing water and discovered the waterfalls for which Edessa is renowned. At one point, it was possible to follow a little path and walk behind the falling water. There is something captivating about falling water for me, or any moving water. It draws me in. I could sit and watch it for hours.

After Edessa we passed through Florina and drove on up to Prespa. On the way we passed by a lake called Vegoriti and ate at a taverna which was called "Friend of God." We had stopped at the café opposite on the shore of the lake - however it was very full of loudly conversing and smoking Greeks. The little taverna, on the other hand, was empty. As well as enjoying excellent but simple food, we were treated to free coffees after our meal having pointed out that we had identical coffee cups at home. Very welcome considering the cold weather which had just descended (or rather, into which we had just ascended).

We drove up to the tiny village of Agios Germanos, which our friendly patron had recommended to us. We were spurned at the door of the only hotel (very biblical), and drove down a little way to the village of Lemos. There we found a very old farm house – not a stable - where we were offered a room. These rooms were heated by small wood burning stoves - at about 850 metres above sea level it apparently gets extremely cold here at night. The tiny bathroom, devoid of any heating, had a bare concrete floor and a makeshift shower head. Its hot water was also provided by a small stove under the tank. Very rustic.

Tuesday 29th April

We spent the day in Prespa. Glorious sunshine welcomed us from our not-too-comfortable night's sleep and so we made an early start on a drive around the lake of Micro Prespa. Pofi had great fun running free in the farmland around the lake and astounded us by voluntarily jumping into the car each time we set off (this was unheard of - the normal procedure was an embarrassing manual installation much against her will). As we drove along, two pelicans gracefully sailed across the lake to their nesting sites. We were informed by the very friendly and helpful girl in the tourist information hut that Micro Prespa was home to the largest flock of pelicans in the world. They were, for the most part, hiding very well.

Wednesday 30th April

Took a little boat to the island of Agios Achillios in the lake of Micro Prespa. Spent a good couple of hours walking around the island and looking in the ruins of an old church with still-visible remnants of frescoes adorning some of its weather-beaten walls. Also spent an hour waiting for the boat guy to decide to come back and pick us up. The guide-book said something about a 'nominal' fee for this service. They should take another look.

Thursday 1st May

We left the Prespa region behind us today, feeling sure we would one day come back. We stopped briefly in Kastoria, but it was much to citified for our liking after the seclusion of the lake. We drove a little loop of tiny villages near Agios Orestiko, principally because the map showed the site of some hot-water springs. There was a trickle of sulphurous-smelling water and a weird set up of old bath tubs lined up in what was little more than a derelict cattle shed. There were ripped and dirty shower curtains hanging between each tub. The mud floor was strewn with debris. Maybe they hadn't opened for the season yet! I wouldn't have bathed the dog in there, let alone myself.

Moving on, we tracked down a place called Nostimo which is apparently the site of a huge petrified forest. The only thing we saw was a tiny museum housed in the local school building, where some artefacts were on display. To be fair, they did say that the site was still being developed and would be open to the public soon. The petrified tree stumps in the playground looked bizarrely alien.

On the summit of an imposingly desolate mountain, we came across the town of Siastita. I have never seen anything like it: miles from anywhere, Siastita had once been the seat of great power in the region. There are numerous rambling old mansions, like something out of colonial India. They are painted in blues and oranges, and have frescoes and gloriously detailed stained glass windows. It must have been a wealthy aristocratic town in its prime. Most of the buildings were in disastrous state of repair, although there was evidence of their being slowly restored. Fascinating place though: we spent hours there.

Finally looking for a room again, we trekked on and found the little village of Nimfeao. Perched high on the top of a murderously winding and climbing mountain road, the village was a lot twee, very tourist orientated, but undeniably beautiful. But for the long drive back down the mountain, we might have moved on. The huge double bed, the white lace bedspread, the whirlpool bath, the central heating: these things conspired to keep us here for the night. Abigail's enjoying the whirlpool now. Qualms about leaving the dog in the car have been overcome; she'll live.

Friday 2nd May

We left in the early morning, guilt about the dog resurfacing, and re-visited Edessa for breakfast. Then on to Loutra, to see some more baths. I was decidedly unimpressed with the idea, memories of the last hovel we had driven to see. This was something else, however. It was like finding a Pontins Holiday Camp in the middle of the Australian outback, after a nuclear war. Virtually in the middle of nowhere, where maybe a sleepy little hamlet ought to have been, was a huge complex of rooms, bars, restaurants and saunas. But very primitive, rustic in the extreme. And closed. We were able to convince the old guy who was care-taking the place to open up one of the baths for us to have a hot soak. Swimming naked in a chest-deep pool of gently bubbling, sulphurous water. Outside, we could see our breath; inside, 37 degrees. The illicit pleasure of nudity in a semi-public place (were there any public) – a magical, if surreal, memory.

Much refreshed, we found a room in nearby Loutraki. Tired of taverna food by this stage, we raided the local mini-market (woefully inadequate corner shop, by any other name) and cooked for ourselves.

I spent most of the evening reading, while Abigail took the dog for a walk around the village and wrote postcards. Tomorrow, we're going to drive all the way back to Athens in time to have a weekend to unwind, and unpack, before the summer term is upon us. We'd originally planned to visit Pella and Ancient Dion on the way home, but we're both all 'antiquitied' out.

Saturday 3rd May

Received a letter from Rachel today. Abigail registered the fact, but didn't enquire further. I felt exceedingly awkward. She has rarely displayed jealousy, so I'm probably projecting my own feelings. Rachel is planning to come to Greece for a month this summer. I'm pleased. We need to talk.

Sunday 4th May

The Monday morning blues have started early. I am not going to be stuck in this job forever. Silent promise to self.

Monday 16th June - Thursday 26th June

The week got off to a good start, with no school on Monday. We spent the day, as the two before, in Spetses. Much sun and swimming. Then the 'it' started - the indefinable 'it' which has permeated the last fortnight.

On Monday evening at about 9.00pm, on the way back home, the police stopped me on my bike. They took the *avia*, that is the registration document, and the number plates, because the bike had no current tax disk. They were, at least, happy with my driving licence. This was bad enough in itself, but Abigail seemed to think that I should in some way have stopped the three huge and heavily armed policemen from taking the plates. She was adamant that the bike was now for the scrap heap, that we would never get the plates back because of all the dodgy paperwork and that it was all my fault. I don't know why she got so worked up about it. After a pointless half hour listening to her literally rave on about it, we left to go home. I dropped her off at her house and went back to my place in a foul mood. She phoned me at two a.m. to see if I'd got back alright. School next day.

With four days to go until the end of term, the Head tells me she still doesn't know if my request to teach another year group can be met. I will not stay in Reception again: I'd go out of my mind. If she doesn't come up with the goods, I will resign.

On Tuesday morning, I arrange to have some time off to go to the tax office to try to get a new sticker for the bike and to pay a fine, so that I can go back to the police station in Corinth and reclaim the number plates for the bike. Abigail says I have no chance, being characteristically negative about the whole thing. They told me that the papers I had for the bike showed it to be registered in Marousi, not Kifissia.

So, on Wednesday morning I again arrange to have time off, less enthusiastically granted this time, it has to be said. I arrive at the right building, eventually find the right floor - nothing is sign-posted - only to find that the vehicle registration department is closed every Wednesday.

Thursday morning at the tax office, now seriously trying the patience of management at work, I find that there is no easy legal way I can get the paperwork I need. Once again, I have to pass myself off as the American doctor who registered the bike. I have to make up both a passport number and a tax number for this guy, having no idea what combinations of numbers and letters are required. I sign various papers (in Greek, so I have no clue what I'm signing) in a false name and am not asked for any proof of ID. I finally pay a fine and get my hands on a bloody tax sticker. It is a 4cm square piece of green paper, worth less than four quid. All of this in over forty-three degrees. 'Hot' doesn't begin to describe it.

Friday is the last day of school. As last year, no real joy, just relief. Spent a couple of hours at the pool, which was unbelievably busy, what with the ridiculous temperatures. Two kids took a thermometer onto the playground this morning at eleven o'clock and came back with a reading of 49 degrees centigrade.

On Saturday we went to the pool for a couple of hours, but felt little like socialising. Our plan was to do something afterwards, but Abigail is starting to feel unwell, something with her stomach. It could just be the heat.

Sunday, and Abigail is definitely unwell. We stay in all day, avoiding the heat, doing nothing in particular. It is too hot to do anything. At about six, she goes up to her place to clean up a bit, and I follow her up at about nine. She has done nothing, is in bed, and feels much worse.

On Monday morning, at 6am, we get up and drive to Corinth. It is already unbearably hot in the car. It takes us until nine to find the right police station. I go in and make my request in faltering Greek. I am gob-smacked! In less then five minutes, I have my plates back. I feel empowered to have been through a load of Greek bureaucracy and emerged victorious. Abigail sleeps in the back of the car on the way back, feeling sick and clearly very uncomfortable. She sleeps on and off all day. At about 9.30 we go to bed at her place. Half an hour later I get up, ride the bike back to my flat to pick up her car, drive back to hers to pick her up, and we go down to the hospital in Marousi. We arrive at the hospital at midnight, having driven there tortuously slowly, because Abigail has such pains in her stomach. We get back to my place at 2.30 in the morning with no clear diagnosis, but appendicitis 'probably' ruled out. She has had some medication, some blood tests and a pain relieving injection. We sleep.

7.30 the next morning: we're up again and back to the hospital for an appointment with the gastroenterologist - still inconclusive. We're there for three hours, none-the-less, trying to chase up the paperwork we need for the insurance company. She also sees a surgeon, who suggests that, whilst it is not full blown appendicitis, it could be a grumbling appendix. Aren't there tests for this kind of thing? Not very reassuring stuff.

We drop off all the relevant insurance papers on the way home, which is a hassle, but cuts out the woefully inefficient middle man. We get back to Anixi to find that Rabbi, one of the cats, has cut his paw somehow, and a significant portion of it is threatening to detach itself most inconveniently from the rest of the cat. We have again left the car at my flat. I again take the bike down to my flat, bring the car back, so we can take the cat, in the car, to the vet. The vet's place is like a scene from a 'B' class horror film. There is a dead dog on the operating table. There is an alarmingly long streak of blood across the floor. The vet is either oblivious or indifferent. He handles the cat very roughly, and gives him a general anaesthetic. He starts to stitch the paw while the cat is evidently still conscious and feeling pain. As we carry the now unconscious form of the patient back to the car, we vow never to go back.

We had planned to go to Skopelos on Monday. Monday became Wednesday. Abigail was bringing the kittens (Artakti and Xionati - Rascal and Snow-White would be very rough translations) from my place up to Anixi where they were to be fed while we were away, when she had to stop at a red light. She'd left her window open because of the heat, and Xionati made a leap for freedom.

I get a frantic call from Abigail and join her in a fruitless search for the cat. At least Rabbi seems to have recovered. We are now minus one animal in our menagerie. Wednesday evening sees us going to bed, not to Skopelos; it was not meant to be.

On Thursday morning it is no longer sunny, which is a relief after temperatures of around 44 degrees in the last few days. Abigail seems better, with medicines, although we still have no idea what the problem is. On Thursday evening, the 'seeming better' proves fallacious, and we are going nowhere. Artakti has now gone AWOL, which fits the current pattern well. Two false alarms today: one for each kitten. Still no sign of either. I am reminded of Kaltsoula's disappearance last year, and wonder what they are trying to tell me!

My motorbike was stolen from outside my flat. Maybe my guardian angel has forestalled a fatal crash. Positive thinking can do wonders. The glass-half-empty / glass-half-full syndrome. I went to the police station to report it, delicately skirting over the 'bike-not-legally-in-my-name' issue, only to be told that I would have to keep an eye out for it. The two guys at the desk did at least note the details and take my phone number. As I was leaving, I understood enough of their little exchange in Greek to gather that they thought it would probably be on its way to an island by now.

And out of all this running around, worrying about Abigail and hoping she'll be alright, surfaces the old fear that all is for nought. I'm tired, helpless, hopeless. I'm stuck, I can't move forward, I've forgotten how.

> *Smiling familiarity*
> *Inviting me down*
> *To that place I know so well*
> *Listless, directionless, meaningless.*
> *The beckoning finger,*
> *Mocking me,*
> *Thinks I have no strength to fight*
> *Often it's right.*
> *The strength I draw*
> *To resist*
> *Still comes from her*
> *Too often, it seems*
> *Somewhere in me*
> *There exists the will*
> *To smilingly decline the offer*

And, on my own, follow another path.
So if it does exist within me, why can't I find it now?

Friday 27th June

Trust, faith and hope
Combined in a vision
Of a future being forged
An inner growth
A slow awakening
Finally realising potential.
In the other world
Which we explain as dreams
We are each awaited
By the waiting one
Patient and understanding
Knowing how difficult it is for us.
The love we are shown
Unquestioning and pure
Lifts us to higher places where
We can know beauty
And can share and revel in
Its truth.
We understand so little
Hoping to know so much
And yet fail to learn
To let go of our fears
Rise above our preconceptions
And know ourselves.

I start my Greek language course next week, on Wednesday. I don't feel ready to do anything of the sort. I feel I need to sleep for a week. Abigail is still not well, and I am worried about her. I feel I need to get away from here. I feel I need to get away from her. But I can't. I need to be with her. I simply need her, and this is becoming too much.

I have decided that I cannot do this any more. Not without help. I have made inquiries about finding an English-speaking counsellor or therapist. If I survive this summer, I'm going to see a psychiatrist in September. This is not about Abigail, and my wanting this relationship to work: well, not only. This is beginning to be about me, and my sanity. This permanent battle in my head is too much for me to manage; right now, it is one I am losing.

> *I am tired of this nonsense in my head*
> *I do not sense the tiredness in my head*
> *Tiredness, nonsense, head*
> *Interchangeable*
> *Head, nonsense, tired*
> *Nonsense?*
> *Head tired*
> *Dead tired*
> *Dead.*

I think I need some time on my own...

Saturday 2nd August - Sunday 10th August

Another disappointing summer so far. We seem too tired to enjoy one another's company. I have learnt, at least, not to force it when it doesn't work, but it's definitely not working. Again. Am I flogging a dead horse? We are as far apart as we have ever been. We don't seem to be able to talk about anything. Sexually, it's a desert. Why can it never be simple and straightforward? This is a relationship beyond hope. I'm trying too hard. I see the damage I am doing. I see my trying becoming desperate. I see me pushing away the person I am trying to get close to. I see me defeating myself. It's time to be alone.

I took the 5pm ferry – The Penelope A - from Rafina. It took twelve hours to get to Amorgos. I slept between islands, waking each time to the announcements of impending arrivals: Andros, Tinos, Mykonos, Syros, Paxos, Naxos and, finally, Amorgos. The boat journeyed on to Crete, I think.

The little port of Katapola bustled as the ferry arrived, but soon calmed after it had left the bay. We were met by locals vociferously offering rooms: "Very cheap. The best prices for you, my friend." I wasn't about to find and pay for a room at five in the morning, so I left them all to it, and went a little way along the port to the beach, where I hoped to be able to sleep until daylight. Circling the bay, the typical Cycladic white box houses shone out against the blackness under a three-quarter moon. I was woken a couple of hours later by the baying of a donkey on the road above me. I had slept on a thin strip of beach, no more than two metres from the sea to the raised road behind. I am immediately reminded of Lipsi as I discover I have shared by brief dreamtime with a family of six white ducks. I am reminded of Abigail too, now far away in France, and the pain of missing her, of wondering if we will be together again, re-surfaces. But I push it away: I am here for me, to unlearn dependency, to find more of myself. On the whole, I am feeling calm, happy to be here, to be away - yet inextricably sad.

Breakfast of espresso and a very greasy croissant - here in Katapola, they know about Athens prices. This is not going to be a cheap island. Have also hired a trials bike, a Yamaha 250cc, for the week. Again, not cheap, but I don't want to be stuck in one place.

It is mid-afternoon and I'm writing from a taverna in Aigali. Three very English-looking boys, aged around ten, are going from table to table asking for unwanted bread. They want to go fishing with it. (That's something amazing in port-side tavernas. You can throw bread into the sea and within seconds there is a thrashing and writhing reminiscent of the piranha scenes in old Tarzan films.) Without exception, they are given a piece of bread from each table; they leave with triumphant smiles, having amused the taverna clientele in the process. I am always impressed by kids doing things I wouldn't have dared to do at their age. Nothing too daring, perhaps, about asking for unwanted bread; perchance I was abnormally shy.

It was amazingly busy last night! Nobody wanted to serve one person sitting alone at a table. The food, when it eventually came, was crap: re-heated, and then only just. Cheap though, and a good retsina.

It's amazing what you begin to notice whilst sitting for hours on your own. Couples, irritatingly enough. Clinging to one another, motor-bike riding, shopping, trying on rings, lying on the beach, pushing each other in the water. So idyllic, so full of hope. Reality bites.

From the village above the port, two old, capped Greeks have arrived. On donkeys. Each beast is additionally burdened with harness, ropes and an empty half barrel. As the riders greet fellow locals and accept the magically-appearing ouzo, the donkeys stand side by side on the beach in the full glare of the overhead sun, now to be petted and photographed by German bikers. (That makes a better photograph: the two loaded donkeys and the two packed Yamahas. Unfortunately it's a photo destined never to be taken, as the German bikers won't move out of the shot.)

I see the moon, large and bright, and want to swim, but am reminded of her. I see a guy change the lens on his camera and am reminded of her. I see a couple playing tavli and am reminded of her. I close my eyes to avoid such images, and in the seclusion of my head, I am reminded of her. This is going to be harder than I thought.

It is afternoon in the white-washed village of Langada, nestled against the mountainside to the north of Aigali. Apparently, the view of the sunset from here is spectacular. The joy of island life is having the time to do this. To arrive in a near-deserted village mid-afternoon, my only plan being to wait for the sunset. Somewhere inside the taverna "*H Loxa*", an old guy is playing the *oute*, a kind of banjo-cum-ukulele. Outside, lining the wall of the café opposite, sit seven guys in their sixties – walking-sticks, caps, komboloi (worry beads). They are seemingly oblivious to the marvel of the live music, not moving, not talking, just 'being'. I could sit here for hours. Part of me wishes I were invisible, so as to observe and to blend into the background, whilst part of me craves company of any kind. Across the *platia*, seeming incongruously modern and alien, a telephone rings…

OK, so the sunset was spectacular. Well worth five hours sat in idle contemplation. I'm now at yet another taverna, waiting for yet another Greek salad, yet another saganaki and yet another portion of chips. What a diet. Not forgetting the indispensable, the obligatory, the life-giving Amstel. Perhaps I'm spending too much time on my own.

> *Solitude*
> *Amongst throngs of people*
> *My body existing here*
> *And now.*
> *My thoughts,*
> *In another time and place,*
> *Turn less and less*
> *To regrets*
> *But to fondness*
> *At what was*
> *But can no longer be.*
> *Sadness exists still*
> *Pervading my now*
> *For now*

I had to be up this morning, Sunday, by ten. I had arranged yesterday to meet at the diving centre. I was awake at seven though, and went down to watch the port come alive. This is a beautiful part of the day. The port itself takes on the characteristics of a life. Sounds begin to appear. The all too familiar cry of a seagull, the fishing boats coming in to port, the isolated voices greeting one another. Movement and sounds: two distinct and separate entities merging. Subtly at first, then more clearly, smells permeate the air. I smell fresh coffee.

This was, however, a cruel trick of my imagination - the instant coffee and overcooked toast I received did not sit well with my romantic image of the awakening port! After my disappointing breakfast, I walked the length of the beach and back, and met not another soul.

Meeting the other divers - 6 people altogether - was an explosion of company after three days of self-imposed isolation. The dive was superb. We were taken out about half a kilometre from the shore where we dived from the boat not far from a small protrusion of rock, too small to be called an island. Eighteen metres below the surface, we were led to the inviting opening of a large cavern, spectacularly lit from above by dramatic rays of sunlight streaming through fissures in its ceiling. The water was crystal clear, and cold, and teaming with fish: I felt as though I were in a Jacques Cousteau film!

Now, at 2 pm, back in my room, the solitude hits me again. I am almost constantly thinking of her, why this is happening, why we are doing this, whether there is any hope at all left for us, whether I want to pursue her any more, how I can step forwards in my life, with or without her. This will take a long time to get over. I look at women around me and cannot imagine being with anyone else. All that work, over again, and for what? To discover two years later that it doesn't work anyway?

Life seems spiteful and cruel to me right now - I want no part of it. I have an absurd notion in my head. Maybe we are all here because we have already sinned. Maybe this is actually a step below our previous existence and is punishment for forgotten wrongs. Who is really happy? And for how long? Or maybe we should simply accept that our lot is not to be happiness, cast the Hollywood dreams aside, and revel in the brief moments of joy that do come our way. 'Seize the day', and all that. Live for the present. But isn't that nihilism? I'm scared of becoming cynical all over again. I don't want to have to close up again to survive. She taught me in a matter of a few weeks how to trust someone and how to feel that intimacy and closeness were possible. I don't want to have to unlearn this lesson in order to move on with my life.

I find that slowly, as I delve into my 'self', I am less and less sad and more and more angry. I am angry at myself for allowing my life to come to this. I have allowed another person to occupy the largest space in my life, to be more important than myself, to be my one true love and my best friend. I see now the vacuum that her leaving my life would leave behind: I am scared that I cannot be these things for myself. I am angry at her, for not just letting me love her, for not just accepting that she is loved, for making this more complicated than it needs to be, for having a past which makes her thus...

After a discouraging taverna meal last night, I had a couple of beers and an early night. I felt suddenly overwhelmed by the meaninglessness of my being here. What am I doing? What do I hope to achieve here? Am I running from my demons again? Have I not learnt that they are within me, that they follow me? Of course I have. I'm just choosing the battle ground.

I must have woken very early again, because after slowly packing and lying on the bed to read for what seemed like a couple of hours, I left my room at 10 o'clock. I found a small beach at Agia (or Saint) Anna. I have investigated its sleeping potential and I think it's OK. There is a tiny canteen nearby, but I can't imagine it getting busy. The beach looks great for snorkelling, very rocky in the water - maybe I'll come back in the early evening and bring some food with me.

Colours floating by
As night sky
Devours day
The first lights are born
Dead before they arrive
False hope
The eye casts upwards
Marvels at its insignificance
And weeps
Here for nought
Or for all?
Here for now!

I'm writing with the fading light on Agia Anna beach. I had chosen the local chapel courtyard to sleep in, but between going to get my gear off the bike and coming back, two people had pinched it! So the beach it is. I'm about five metres from the sea, behind a large rock. I've collected a couple of armfuls of driftwood, made a small rock windbreak, and now I'm just waiting for the dark to signal my lighting of the fire. I bought bake rolls, a banana, some feta cheese and a small bottle of ouzo. I feel alive. Sun-burnt, I'm beginning to notice; sweaty and salty; hungry, but alive.

This solitude has made me realise how mentally and soulfully tired I am. I feel I have been giving and giving. I'm in danger of having nothing left to give, of feeling nothing for her, and I never want to do that. My giving, however, has carried with it unvoiced expectations of receiving. It doesn't work like that. I have to learn to give of myself, to give for the sake of giving, to give because it's what I really want to do, irrespective of any imagined or perceived outcome. I'm going to finish Sebastian Faulkes' "Birdsong" in what's left of the light.

As I sat on an outcrop of rock overhanging the sea and watched the full moon rise and, one by one, the stars appear, I thought, "Nothing else could be this beautiful". I felt tranquil and I liked being me, being where I was: I was enjoying my now. Now, this morning, as I sit on the same rock and watch the sun emerge from its nocturnal bed of sea, I again think, "Nothing else could be this beautiful." And as the sun warms me, I can think of nowhere else I'd rather be and of no-one I would want to intrude on my solitude. Am I learning to like being with me?

My windbreak worked. When I got up in the morning, I was almost blown over. My little sleeping niche was calm and sheltered though. I thought I'd heard voices and footsteps in the night - this morning the two people who had slept (or rather, had tried to sleep) in the little church courtyard were sleeping in the cove next to mine. They didn't look comfortable. I can imagine the night they'd had. I was reminded of the long, sleepless night Abigail and I had spent at a similar chapel last summer. The memory came back to me as a happy one, not tinged at all with sadness. This is happening to me more and more often.

Evening falls slowly. Katapola is almost two distinct settlements: one across the bay from the other. As I sit in this taverna, I watch lights flicker to life opposite me. I can see the room I found this morning. The old woman who showed it to me was very concerned that I was on my own.

She thought the room would be too expensive for one person. She said the price of the rooms was five thousand drachmas. I hadn't the heart to tell her how cheap her rooms were. Maybe I should have. As we climbed hundreds of steep steps to the top of the hill overlooking the harbour, I was very concerned about the old woman. I'm not totally unfit, but I'm glad I don't have to do that walk every day of my life. How she manages it at her age is a mystery to me. Must be all that olive oil.

This island is growing on me. I'd like to stay longer. I have the very beginnings of an idea to come and stay for a month next year - to write. Just to be able to sit and do nothing, to put pen to paper when the inspiration comes. I'm dreaming, of course, since I have nothing but time on my hands now and find it increasingly hard to concentrate on anything other than Abigail. Who am I kidding? I've just finished half a litre of retsina, which is taking effect very quickly since I have eaten nothing today. The wind is beginning to pick up again, and is howling and whistling like the soundtrack from an old horror film.

"Birdsong" was exquisite. It was all I could do not to turn from the last page back to the first and begin again. Having enjoyed 'Freedom and Death' by Kazantzakis, I bought "The Last Temptation" today. I had reservations though, recalling the controversy which the film of the same had provoked, and wondering whether I would enjoy it at all. Now, halfway through, I am enthralled by this vision of a struggling Christ. I am reminded of Bach's "Illusions" too. I find my self identifying strongly. This is rather worrying.

Gazing into the growing darkness, the mountains shrouded in drifting cloud, the wind moaning its mournful songs, I am gripped by an immense feeling of well being. I have always feared following my desire to write, because I've feared the solitude that writing must surely bring. I have discovered, however, that I can do this. Solitude is not impossible for me; I can bear my own company. It would be truly ironic, if in finding me, I lose Abigail. I am beginning to feel, however, that that might be a price worth paying. Strange, how the world turns. I had thought that I would be scared of it turning this way - and I am - but it already feels like a new beginning. With or without her, my life is entering a new and positive phase. I have her to thank for so much of this. It would be just too poignant if she weren't around to see it!

I am a free spirit
Beautiful and loving
Emanating light.
In my eagerness
For her to see it
I stumble and fall
Extinguishing my light
Renting my gowns
Tarnishing my beauty.
And so she sees
My eagerness as desperation
My love as fear
I become less than I am
And she sees the sadness
With which this false image fills me
But I am a free spirit
Beautiful and loving
Emanating light
She will see it
Of her own accord,
In time

Saturday morning - it's good, having to work out what day it is. An intense recognition of freedom! This is what life is all about. Moments. Magical moments of inspiration, of enlightenment, or just of peace.

Totally overcast this morning - it makes an interesting, and not entirely unwelcome, change. I am again surrounded by French. In the street, I hear as much French spoken here as I do Greek. Two French girls have just left my table. I saw them on the beach yesterday, watching me surreptitiously as I read. This morning, one of them asked if they could join me, although there were other tables free. I answered her English with French. There was a bizarre exchange as we both struggled in each other's language for a while. Then we managed a conversation of sorts, relying more strongly on her English than my French. Was I alone? Where was I from? Really? I lived in Athens? Wow, that must be so exciting! She was nice, pretty, friendly. Remy, she's called, and Nadine, her silent friend. Both in their early twenties. Casual sex being offered on a plate. Not interested. She'll see me around, she says. And was that a wink, or did I imagine it? Definite unsolicited hand (hers) to upper arm (mine) contact as she left. Why am I not interested?

I am drawn so strongly to the sound of that language though. Clearly associations with Abigail. When I try to objectively (ha!) way up the pros and cons of being with her, I have two distinct lists in my mind. The cons consist of reality, selfishness, loss of self: the pros float on dreams, feelings, hopes and desires. Head and heart in conflict. So: to seek refuge in aloofness, reasoning and calculation? Or to risk the pains of love, sensitivity and dreams? Why can't I decide what I want? And, as much I hate to admit it, thoughts return to Rachel. She'll be in Athens next week. Is it time to make a decision?

Back in the solitude of my room, unable to sleep, my mind pours over possibilities. An image in my head of making love to Abigail, both of us in tears, refuses to go away. Why, why do I have to torture myself? What will be will be. I wrote once, when I first met Abigail, "Has she demons of her own which will bring us both down?" How prophetic. How pathetic: why do I not learn to trust my intuition? I recognise that it is not just my failing to love positively, but her failing to accept being loved. So why do I not just bail out now? Because I feel something stronger. I feel a connection with her that I cannot explain. Our lives are inextricably linked by a force greater than our fears or our loves. And I do love her and I do fear her.

What cruel Jester's trick is this? (And why have I come over all Shakespearean?) Time refuses to pass today. I've been back to my room, but was unable to sleep. Showered, read, wrote a little, tried to pass time. Now I'm out again and thinking it must be six o'clock or so and that I'll have a beer somewhere, and eat. It's only half past four. The port of Katapola is in siesta mode and I'm sitting on a bench watching a warship leave the harbour, feeling the afternoon sun on my chest.

And still the day drags on. A few beers and a little food later, and it's only eight o'clock in the evening. The sun has disappeared beneath the horizon and the sky is glowing red. I find I am looking forward to leaving tomorrow. To leaving, or to seeing her? A good question. In some respects I dread seeing her. Maybe because while I don't actually see her, dreams can still live. Who wants reality?

I am definitely now receiving odd looks from other tables: my writing seems to unnerve people. At times, it unnerves me. I woke up many times in the night. In all I've had a very restless twenty four hours. I dreamt vividly. I was in a new flat (mine, I think) with Mark, a friend from university days. I don't remember what we were doing, but the flat felt new. Joanne was there - she had her own room in the flat. She asked me, a little sarcastically, if her boyfriend could stay the night. I remember feeling bothered at first, but then realised it was nothing to do with me anyway. Mark and I settled in early to watch something on TV, and Joanne was getting ready for bed in her room. I thought it was odd that she was not going out. In the morning, she asked if her boyfriend could borrow the motorbike. There was some confusion about his taking it: I was telling Joanne I needed it back in two hours but she didn't appear to be listening. They didn't come back until the following morning. I was furious, but she was laughing. I hit her hard across the face and she fell into the bath. I turned on the water.

Sunday morning. Tonight I go back to Piraeus. So how do I feel about going back, seeing Abigail again? She should have come back from Paris yesterday. I promised I would phone her, but I haven't. It's been hard at times to resist calling, but I felt I needed complete isolation from her. So how do I feel? Scared of what I will feel? Or of what I won't feel?

I do love the early mornings on the islands. It is just after 9 o'clock and there is only a handful of people about. I'm sitting in the sunshine at the '*Aeginon*' awaiting coffee and a croissant. This time tomorrow I'll be home. Home. What a plethora of images that word can conjure. Right now, a home without Abigail wouldn't feel at all homely. I'm remembering the Billy Joel song, "You're my home". How wrong we are to invest another person with such power! Everything in our culture directs us to it. It's as though we are on self-destruct from the beginning. Eternal love, the 'one' person who can make you happy, 'happily ever after' - it's all such bullshit. We're basically here on our own to make the best of it, to learn and to grab what companionship or happiness come our way for as long as they last. Hopes and dreams grow into expectations and explode in our faces. They rob us of our present by dangling a glittering future that never arrives. We have to invest ourselves in our now. Who the fuck am I preaching to?

I'm now back in Aigali. It's about eleven thirty. I seem to have become extremely obsessed with time over the last couple of days. It's because I've run out of books to read and the weather's no good for sitting on the beach. Too windy. It has become too cold to go far on the bike: the mountains are covered in clouds. On some daft impulse, I've bought Abigail a pair of silver earrings.

I've just realised, after a week, that I have not noticed one other person on his own: not on the beach, not eating, not just having coffee. No-one. Maybe it's just me! I wouldn't mind a game of *tavli* for a change. The empty café I sat at to have yet another coffee is now full. All couples, I might add. The sky is really clouding over, it could even rain. If I could fast-forward to tonight, I certainly would. So much for living in the now.

Having tried the beach for a couple of hours, I have resorted to ice-cream and coffee. Serious self-counselling coming up. When I feel depressed, it is *my* emotion, which *I* create. Outside factors influence me, but the choice to feel this way is MINE. I am choosing differently now. I'm not in denial. If Abigail and I can't work things out, I shall grieve, I shall be sad. But I shall not be inconsolable. Nobody has the power to destroy my life but me. I feel good about myself. My sadness is for her, what she's losing out on, as well as for me. On my own, life will seem empty for a while, because she has been such a large part of it. Not that, of course, we are inevitably finishing. If we do, though, life will seem directionless for a while, because she has been my direction. I shall feel lost, because in so many things, she has been my compass. But I will not feel despair. I have a life to live, love to give, and the capacity to enjoy my life.

It's cold and windy. I'm wearing shorts and a vest, eating ice-cream and drinking cold coffee. Why?

I wonder how much I'm in love with the idea of being in love with her? The reality is never as good as the illusion I create when she's not with me. So being with her must be almost continually disappointing. My God, I've been asleep for so long! Wake up!

It's just hit me like a bolt from the blue. I've even taken a photo of the place of my inspiration. I feel inexpressibly happy. I'm walking in Langada, in the mountains. I've spent most of the last year waiting. My life has been on hold. One way or another I've been waiting for Abigail. Either literally to come home or to call me or, more generally, waiting for her to accept being loved. For the first time since I met her, I feel free of her. I feel unburdened and light. No matter what happens, whether we try to stay together or finally part, I have taken from her the power to hurt me. This doesn't mean I don't love her or want to be with her. I've found a part of myself that is strong. A part of me I didn't know I had. And now I have so strong a grip on it that I'm sure I'll never lose it so completely again.

144

I am going to try again with Abigail. I have the strength to change where I need to and I have discovered self-direction. I hope she doesn't pass this up - for her sake as well as for my own. I'm going to be OK.

I have never truly believed this before.

A sunset, the slight sensation of sunburn on my face, the sound of the waves caressing the shoreline, a cold beer to hand. Who am I to demand more than this from life? Would I want to share this moment with anyone? No. It is mine, and with it, within my 'now', I am truly happy. I think God touched me today, and life begins again. I fell in love with the idea of her. I created her: her age, her nationality, her experience, her uniqueness. They were all part of her, but not her. The real her could only ever disappoint and hurt me. What immense pressure I have been putting on her. Now I see her for what she is: a beautiful person in pain, struggling in her own way to make sense of life, of all that has happened to her. I have made the mistake of pushing too hard to see all of her pain, thinking I could help, ever trying to 'fix' things. I can't. More importantly, I don't want to. I do want to be with her when she's happy, I do want her to be happy. But I no longer want to share everything: her problems, her fears. I can't solve them. Now I'm going to be selfish, not in a negative way, but in a positive way, for me. I'm the only person I'm prepared to suffer for and I've turned a corner in my life. I want her, but I don't want our old relationship back. I'd love to make love to her, but I don't want to share a bed with her turned back and her infinite sadness. I dreaded feeling this but, now that I do, I can see it as a huge step forward. I do still love her, care about her, think about her; but I no longer crave, need, cling. I'm so glad to be through this. Not that I have any illusions about an easy future. I do, however, have a clearer idea about where I'm going.

I'm sitting on a hard, wooden bench on the 'Penelope A', wrapped in a sleeping bag and leaving the port of Katapola behind me and, with it, the lost and anguished exile who fled Athens a week ago. I am amazed that such a change can come about, be wrought, in just seven days: that I have come to understand and appreciate so much that I simply couldn't see before. Feeling this good is all well and fine but I'm sure she's been doing some thinking of her own. Maybe she's decided that she can't continue with this? If so, I can only tell her how wrong I think she is, and how right I think we can be together.

I don't trust myself to stay this positive on my own, though. I did find the number of an English therapist working in Athens...

Tuesday 12th August

Got back to an empty flat yesterday. Memories of when we used to live here together. New-found strength faltering, like a trembling, splay-legged foal, I decided to spend the day out of the flat. Couldn't face unpacking, so went into Athens on the train. Phoned Abigail's place but no answer, and no messages at mine either. Ominous.

Wednesday 13th August

No answer in France either. I suppose I deserve the silent treatment for not having been in touch with her whilst I was on Amorgos. I went up to her place on the bus to find it locked with a padlock on the garden gate. This is new to me. Climbed into the garden to check that she hadn't actually moved out while I was away. Paranoid? She hadn't.

When I got back to my place, there was a phone message saying she'd be back in Athens tomorrow at ten in the morning. I could pick her up from the airport if I wanted. If I weren't there, she'd take a taxi. So, I went back up to her place, again on the bloody bus, silently cursing the theft of my bike. I climbed the padlocked gate and made for her car keys. I had that tingly, teenager-about-to-go-on-first-date feeling. I felt that the rest of my life could well start tomorrow and was eager for it to arrive. Spent a long time counselling myself about this.

Friday 15th August

A part of me feels that I could end this diary now, with the words 'happily ever after': two years to the day after I started writing it, oddly enough. That's the part of me I'm leaving behind though. I remembered our last euphoric reunion at the airport, only to find that in less than a year that we had again drifted far apart.

The relief at seeing her again, knowing that I still felt so strongly about her, the intense optimism about myself: emotions spilling over one another.

I cannot describe how it is to touch her, and be touched by her. There's a force flowing between us, both electric and spiritual. I can even visualise it, rippling in colours and waves around her body. I felt an urgency yesterday, while we were making love for the first time, to be deep inside her. Not just sexually, but all of me, to wrap myself up in her, with each thrust willing myself to enter into her and become one with her: touching, holding, embracing, penetrating, entwining, enveloping, protecting, protected, needing, needed, loving, loved…

Saturday 16th August

It seems that we have been thinking along very similar lines during our time apart. She tells me that she doesn't want to feel needed, only wanted. Being needed carries an implicit responsibility to provide, to care, to be obliged. These things are all too heavy a burden for her to bear. I can well understand that, given her history. But from me, there came the other side of the coin: she turns from being loved, finds it hard to accept things, material or emotional, is constantly scared of being in some kind of imagined perceived debt. The walls go up; the defences set. Clearly we both have work to do.

Sunday 17th August

Spent the day casually doing nothing. The fish and terrapin have survived our absences, although it is hard to tell if they are pleased to see us. The cats are, at least, pleased to be able to sleep inside at night.

I'm spending more and more time up here. It's peaceful, further removed from the hustle of Kifissia, closer to the rural idyll. I begin to think we should try living together again. It would be cheaper, if nothing else.

Abigail now knows that Rachel is coming. She doesn't seem to have a problem with it. Rachel's intelligent enough not to expect anything and Abigail is convinced that it's better to tempt the devil and find out the truth about life than to hide away. In something of a perverse way, I'd quite like them to meet.

Monday 18th August

No sooner have we arrived than we're off again. It seems appropriate to spend a little time together in a holiday mood, rather than just stay at home(s). The fish and the terrapin and the cats, and the dog this time, will have to cope without us for a couple of days more.

We've borrowed the summer house in Sounion again. It seems strange to be here in such glorious weather, it's upwards of thirty-five degrees. Now that we can venture outside (we didn't leave the bed much, let alone the flat, on our last visit) we can appreciate the spectacular location: we are virtually over-hanging the sea. A braver person than I am might actually manage to jump into the sea from the balcony here, but as it's over twenty metres, I'll give it a miss. There's a rickety-looking ramp way-cum-staircase leading down to a secluded beach, which has no other apparent access point.

It's actually fun to go shopping, buying meagre provisions for our short stay, choosing things together.

Tuesday 19th August

Spent the afternoon on the beach yesterday, swimming, sunbathing, reading, talking. I am not going to again get into the trap of inferring too much by way of perfection into this, but it's pretty bloody good.

Returned to the beach for night-swimming. REM springing unbidden but not unwelcome to my mind. Highly charged erotic interludes seem to punctuate this relationship. I probably couldn't keep it up if it were sustained on a regular basis. There's nothing quite as sensual as the touch of sea water and sand while making love.

This evening, we are going to the monument at Cape Sounion to watch the sunset. Cameras and picnic at the ready.

Wednesday 20th August

I had no idea Sounion was so popular a spot. It was truly difficult to find a place to stand to get only the sunset in the shot, and not hoards of tourists. A spectacular sight though, as the sun turns a deep, majestic red and sinks into the sea, framed by the marble columns of Poseidon's Temple.

Thursday 21st August

Bugger, forgot dad's birthday. Tail-between-legs honesty or plausible lie about the inefficiency of the Greek postage system? I think the first. How noble.

Back home, but the subject of living together not yet broached. Why rock the boat just yet?

Very apologetically phoned dad to explain the non-appearance of birthday card or phone call on the day. He was apparently away at the time anyway, so I could have claimed to have been calling all day. Feel better with the honest approach and he seemed OK with it anyway. Will send something suitably Greek next time I venture into Plaka.

Friday 22nd August

Popped into school today to try to get my head around working there again for another year. Bumped into the Head and she dropped the bombshell on me that I could, after all, have a change of age-group this year. I'll be teaching ten and eleven year olds. That means I have some work to do between now and the first of September. Feel relieved though, and now quite looking forward to starting again. It'll soon wear off.

Sat at the pool for a couple of hours, showing off my Amorgos suntan; I've never been so brown in my life. Or fit. The regime of irregular exercise, plus the stress-related poor dietary habits of the last month, have conspired to lose me a few pounds. Not that I'd recommend it as a way of losing weight. I saw a photo of a red Beetle advertised there and instantly knew I was going to buy it. I do fancy it; there's something classy and full of character about a Beetle. It's a 1965 model. It'll be a bargain if it's in reasonable condition. There's also the added incentive of not spending another winter astride a push-bike! Now that the motorbike has gone, I do need some transport, especially if I move up to Abigail's place: that really is too far to ride. Oh, to be able to arrive in work dry and relaxed!

Saturday 23rd August

I asked Abigail what she would feel about living together again. I said that if we were really going to make a go of it, then I wanted to be with her in every sense, to share the boring stuff, as well as the good stuff. I want to go shopping for kitchen accessories, to have someone else squeeze the toothpaste from the middle of the tube, to wait for the bathroom in the morning, to argue about whose turn it is to wash up. Actually, I want her face to be the last thing I see every night before I drift off to sleep, and for it to be the first thing I see every morning. I want to do it differently this time, without expectations of perfection. I want to enjoy each day for the pleasures it brings, instead of hoping tomorrow will bring something exceptional. I want us to just 'be'- together.

She thought for a few timeless seconds, before breathing, 'Yes'.

Sunday 24th August

> *On living together*
> *Sharing a house*
> *Sharing the mundane*
> *As well as the spectacular*
> *Planning for intimacy*
> *Choosing the chattels*
> *Creating a home.*
> *Guarding the inner spirituality*
> *Looking for expressions*
> *Of outward growth.*
> *Becoming a 'we'*
> *Through the strength and belief in*
> *My 'me'.*
> *My eyes open,*
> *Rose-tinted glasses long since discarded,*
> *Feeling this time it can work.*
> *Another new phase begins:*
> *Talkshop*
> *Assertions of me.*
> *Problems to be faced*
> *Finally emerging*
> *In words.*

Monday 25th August

Went to see the car with Abigail. She thinks it's cute but too expensive for what it is. I'm sure she's right. But I won't find a better deal before term starts, and I don't see her giving me a lift into work every morning. She thought this last point was a good one and urged me to buy it.

Abigail is having stomach pains again. Here we go...

Tuesday 26th August

Today I bought a car. Two years in Greece and I am finally mobile and dry. It's not quite falling apart. Steers like a pig, no road holding at all. Driver's seat collapses backwards at the slightest pressure, so I drive pulling myself forwards by the steering wheel. It's got little push/pull white knobs for the windscreen wipers and the reverse light. A snip at three hundred thousand drachmas. (Well, cars are expensive here, what can I say? Something to do with import protectionism, I think.) It feels so good to be sitting behind a wheel again - it's even got a halfway decent stereo. Well, it plays tapes with sound coming out of both speakers and none of that nasty crunchy, chewy noise which my last car stereo produced as a prelude to eating the tape.

Drove into school and sorted out my classroom. Very easily done, as I have nothing to put in it. I'll have twenty kids in my class. In England, I had thirty-six. Maybe it's possible to actually achieve something with twenty, instead of being there just for crowd control.

Got home to more of the same from Abigail. She has a temperature and is definitely unwell. She has promised to see a doctor tomorrow.

Speaking of tomorrow, I'm meeting Rachel at ten. She's been here a week already, but has been visiting friends on the islands. She sounded as bright and cheerful as ever. She doesn't want to stay at mine, which is actually a relief, as I wasn't sure how I was going to deal with that one. She says she's looking forward to seeing me again. I'm not sure how I feel. Actually, that's not true – I'm looking forward to seeing her too. It's just that I feel awkward about it. I know I love this woman. She knows it too. And yet, she also knows about Abigail and vice versa. Interesting. She definitely wants to talk about something specific, I can feel it.

Wednesday 27th August

Rachel is getting married! I knew there was something. I spent a wonderful morning with her, and will meet her fiancé later this week too. He's a Greek-Australian, which didn't surprise me. I'm actually happy. Yes I do love her, and that also means wanting her happiness. We kissed, perhaps a bit more passionately than either of our respective partners would have approved of. We knew what we were doing. There are times when just good friends, very good friends, is actually quite magnificent.

I got back home from this rendezvous to discover that Abigail has appendicitis. She is having her appendix removed this afternoon. At the same hospital that said she didn't have appendicitis last time around. One has to wonder at the timing.

Today I gave my notice to the landlord, who professed to being very sorry to see me go. So sorry that he reckons he's keeping my three month deposit as forfeit, because I'm breaking my contract, which was for three years. I never signed any contract. I also never got a receipt for the three month deposit. *Malaka!* Having asked around, this appears to be fairly standard practice. Doesn't make it feel any better.

Phoned the therapist in Athens. She has just returned from holiday and starts on Monday. I made an appointment for next Wednesday evening. Now I'm scared.

Thursday 28th August

Left my natty little motor with a garage to service it and have two new front seats put in. Not new, of course, but salvaged from a Golf. Apparently he can make them fit. Driving with the old seat was really tiring and bloody dangerous. Am stupidly excited about this.

Visited Abigail in hospital to find that she was fit enough to check out and come home with me. I told her when we got home that I am going to start seeing a therapist. I was a little nervous about this and worried about her response. It's something I've decided to do for myself, though, not really needing her approval. I was amazed by how positive she was about it. She understood exactly why I wanted to and felt it would be a very good idea. And then she hit me with it: she'd been in therapy herself, for a couple of years. She asked me if I remembered the boyfriend she was seeing when we first met. I guessed it was a rhetorical question.

Apparently, he was an invention: she wasn't living with anyone. That's why it had been so easy to go in and collect all her stuff. And to think I'd been really nervous about this guy being around. She'd been on her own, or at least not in a serious relationship, for three years. So why the act? She said that she didn't think she could ever want to be with someone again. 'Be with' in terms of sharing intimacy, sharing histories, sharing a life. Why so strong? The 'attempted' suicide she told me about actually took place two years before we'd met, a year to the day that she had split up with him; and the attempt was successful. He left a vitriolic letter, blaming her. At the time, she believed it, accepted the responsibility, and nose-dived into her guilt and pain. No wonder she reacted strongly to her perception of my becoming needy and placing her in the centre of my life! Part of me felt hurt that she had kept this from me for so long. I realised, though, that she was quite probably right. How would knowing this have helped me at all? Would it have made any difference at all? I thought I was the one who had been going through Hell to make this relationship work.

How self-involved am I? I begin to grasp the nature of the demons she has been facing in order to be with me…

Friday 29th August

I'm getting my Beetle today. Abigail doesn't want to come with me as she wants to clean the house, and try to make room for my stuff by re-arranging things. Of course, that's the last thing she should be doing as she has strict instructions to relax and take it easy. Apparently it can take weeks to fully recover from her operation, and she's clearly in pain. (As I'm losing my deposit anyway, we thought I might as well start moving my stuff in right away, little by little each day. We'll have to see if I can chain gang some help from school, as there's no way Abigail can be lugging furniture around with me.)

I'm going out with Rachel and Vangelis later. Abigail has a good excuse not to come, and I genuinely think that she would have if she had been feeling better.

Saturday 30th August

Last night was great. Italian meal, decent wine, but not too much of it. They make a great couple. Vangelis was a bit guarded at first, which is probably understandable, though I don't know quite what she's told him about me. They must have got together just after I visited Rachel in Australia last Christmas. We parted last night in fine form, promising to keep in touch. They are heading back to Australia, but Melbourne this time, which is where he lives. The final squeeze of the hand said more than words could have done. I went back home to my place on a high, phoning Abigail to wish her a good night, to fill her in on the evening's events, and to tell her I loved her.

Picked up my Beetle today. It looks brilliant. Was so proud that I took it round to Richard's and persuaded him to wash it with me. Bought a special red waxy-based thing to do the job properly. Very pleased with the result. Also realistically recognise that it's probably the last time it will get washed. We went for a little spin, and then had a celebratory drink to 'wet the baby's head' and toast Rachel's engagement. Richard had also met and liked Vangelis, though he thinks me a fool for letting Rachel slip away. He didn't get the idea that she would never be away. Had one or three too many, and, very sensibly, phoned Abigail to say I'd be staying at Richard's, and to ask if she was feeling okay. She said she'd be fine and we should have a proper boys' night. Richard found half a bottle of whiskey...

Abigail phoned at about two in the morning, asking if I fancied going to Evia or somewhere for the weekend, and if so, to get back early in the morning. I reminded her that she is supposed to be convalescing and a three hour drive in an old Beetle isn't the best way to do that. Of course, she knows better. Anyway, got back at nine this morning and we're off to Prokopi for the day and night with the dog, the tent and a lot of painkillers...

I can't do this drinking thing any more.

Sunday 31st August

Camped in a beautiful little spot by a river last night. I understood the phrase 'murmuring brook' for the first time. It really sounded as though there were hushed voices talking all night. I went out to investigate at one point, sure that there must be a camp full of gypsies just around the river bend. It was the water though, mumbling happily to itself as it coursed through the undergrowth.

Wednesday 15th October

It is Wednesday night. I've been absent from my diary again. For once, this is more due to the fact that I'm spending time actually living, rather than moping around worrying about living. The last few weeks have been good. Abigail seems completely recovered. She's made of tougher stuff than me; I don't do pain well.

I am starting my third year of teaching in Athens. In England I left behind a dysfunctional family, a broken-hearted ex-girlfriend, and the onset of manic depression. In Greece I found temporary salvation in a new lifestyle and a new relationship. The novelty of the former is fading. The thrill of the latter, although revived in recent weeks, is largely in the past. The relationship is moving on. I love my girlfriend. We have been through the passion of new-found romance, the discovery of personal histories, hopes and dreams gone astray. We have gone through the fears of abandonment, of committal, of rejection. We have separated and found one another again. I have hoped for too much, she for too little. We lived together, lived apart, and now are living together again. An objective rear-view-mirror perspective of the last two years.

154

I play the guitar intermittently, not brilliantly, but well enough for me to enjoy it. I am reading a lot, and taking the time to think about what I read. I am writing more and moving perceptively closer to a decision to do so more seriously. I have learnt to dive and am now speaking serviceable Greek. I have met and fallen in love with a remarkable woman. We are living together, planning a future. All of this in the last two years. It all sounds so positive and strong, and yet...

And yet, I do not recognise myself in what I'm doing. I still see the frightened child within me who wants to be held, who wants to be told he's okay, who wants to be told, "I love you." This weak and needy part of me is less prominent than it was. I know I'm okay, worthy of being loved, talented in some areas, and, at my best, happy with myself. At my worst, I can undo all of this in an instant.

School is just a depressing place to be. This is not surprising. The kids are great: I've got a lively and intelligent group of pupils who get on well together and largely enjoy being in school. When the classroom door is closed and we're working or talking or larking around, I feel that I'm in the right job. The bullshit bureaucracy, however, remains the same, if not worse. I am now daily thanking my lucky stars or guardian angel, or whoever is deserving of my thanks, that I will 'soon' be out of it. I have finally made the decision to step out of teaching for a year, or maybe for good, and give myself time and space to write. Talking about what I really want to do in therapy has been so helpful. I find that teaching gives me less and less satisfaction, but that I'm staying with it because I'm scared to find out what another life would be like. That's crazy. I am again reminded of Bach and his reluctant Messiah: that we are led through our lifetimes by a playful inner self, always free to chose a new future or a different past.

I am not going to be someone who moans 'If only...' when I'm sixty. At least this way I'll find out if there is anything there or if this is just a pipe-dream. The practicalities of surviving here without a job have not yet surfaced as reality. But who cares about practicalities? I can get by on private English lessons, but the actuality of no regular monthly pay check, no medical insurance and no quietly accumulating pension scheme has yet to register. To him who dares...

> *If you are truly unhappy at this moment in time*
> *Doing what you are doing*
> *Then stop.*

Nothing is so important
As to demand
Your unhappiness.
Let go,
Turn around,
Go and do something else.
The only thing keeping you here
Is your fear and your uncertainty
Of the future.
Let go
Of such
Negative emotions.
Learn to see
Fear as challenge,
Uncertainty as adventure.
Learn these things well
And you will
Awaken.
Did you really think
That someone else
Would do this for you?

With this little project in mind, I have bought myself a rather nifty PC, complete with printer and fax modem. It is an interesting toy and I now have access to the Internet. This was a mistake, I think. It is little more than a diversion from what I want to be doing and wastes extraordinary amounts of time. I have yet to receive a phone bill, but expect the worst.

Abigail came good on an old promise which, frankly, I'd forgotten about. I was treated to a private rendition of 'The flight of the bumble bee'! I had been captivated by the scene in 'Shine': Geoffrey Rush's portrayal of David Helfgott's magical version of Rimsky-Korsakov's barely minute-long piece in the café where he has installed himself at the piano. It sounded weird and wonderful on a cello, and the whole ensemble, the music and the purpose behind it, brought tears to my eyes.

Thursday 16th October

For the first time since getting the seats changed on the car, I had reason to try to move them forward to let someone into the back. They don't move! At all! There is no mechanism on them either for adjusting the position of the seat backwards or forwards, or for tilting the seat back.

I drove straight round to the garage, and he casually explained that they were like that because they came from a four-door Golf, and he'd had to weld them into place to get them to fit into my car. No problem. Greeks never fail to amaze me. This guy genuinely thought that this was a perfectly acceptable state of affairs. It was only when I insisted on taking him out to the car and telling him to get into the back that he had any inkling of what was bothering me. In what I'm sure he thought was a magnanimous gesture, he offered me ten thousand drachmas back from the forty I had paid him. Understanding the Greek psyche a little now, and knowing there was no way I would get a better proposition, somewhat surprised at being offered anything, I accepted. Silently fuming.

Wednesday 22nd October

Talked about getting in touch with my anger today. Very clichéd. It's a real problem though. Am I so bothered about everyone else's opinion of me, so needful of their approval, that I can't risk offending or upsetting anyone, even total strangers, for fear of losing their tacit approval? That has been the case, in my past. Now I'm repeating learned behaviour. Unlearning is always hard. Nobody told me it would be this hard, though.

Wednesday 5th November

Uncomfortable silences. Wordless. Non-judgemental. Accepting that nothing-to-say is alright. Guilt for another's time has no place here. Craving another's good opinion, affirmation: no place here. To sit, to think, to not feel the need to apologise, to create for the sake of having something to say. Wordless, but not pointless.

Wednesday 12th November

I've been feeling disheartened these past few weeks, not wanting to be with Abigail particularly, rather enjoying my own company, very much wanting to do my own thing. I have let myself interpret this feeling as a pulling away from Abigail, a weakening of our relationship. In a short hour today, I have shown myself another view.

I am beginning to know and like myself. The work I started on Amorgos has been picked up and continued through therapy. The 'me' I used to lock away, push to the background and discount in favour of other people's opinions and desires is growing into a 'me' I respect and value above other people. This is a totally new concept for me and I have to accept that this will radically alter every relationship I have. Other people (even, or maybe especially, Abigail) do not count as much as they used to. This sounds selfish. Of course they count. But they don't automatically count more than I do. I have found from somewhere a belief in myself. I find I no longer crave approval and feel freer than I have ever felt in my life.

I could have caught the Metro and been home in time to go to the cinema with her. I find now that I don't want to. I'm happier sitting here, drinking coffee, writing in my diary, enjoying being alone. This is not about Abigail, about our relationship, this is about me. I feel better about myself than I have for years. Am I finally putting some of my crap dependency and paranoia behind? I truly think so.

Wednesday 19th November

> *A cool breeze*
> *Blowing through my mind*
> *Birdsong*
> *In my head*
> *The passing minutes*
> *Allies finally*
> *On my side*
> *Not at my back*
> *A certainty,*
> *Not for the future,*
> *The sane cannot have this,*
> *But for the here and now*
> *The infinite calmness*
> *Stillness*
> *With its unique beauty*
> *Bathes within me*
>
> *I am uniquely blessed*
> *Privileged*
> *In my contentment*
> *And in my peace*
> *My searching spirit*
> *After aimless roaming*
> *And myriad follies*
> *Is finding its way*
> *With a confidence*

Never realised before
I see my purpose;
I am home.

Wednesday 26th November

I went to therapy this evening. I exuded happiness and self-confidence. I talked for the whole hour, non-stop. I don't think my therapist said more than ten words herself. I left feeling high, not quite knowing where this spirit of confidence came from. Slowly I have realised that I can make myself, my 'self' that is, happy. I got in touch with this idea on Amorgos. Now it's easier to find again. I no longer rely on Abigail to make me happy. I feel more 'me'. I am beginning to see work, not as the evil interference that I have felt it to be for so long, but as simply something I have chosen to do. It is equally something I can choose not to do. The idea in my head that I am for some reason tied to this job is a fallacy. I can choose to leave at any time. I do not need this sort of money to survive. I suddenly see the future as open once more - full of possibilities, not of restrictions.

Wednesday 3rd December

I am beginning to recognise that the emotions I thought of as loving and caring were possibly not quite either of those things. It was possibly more about control and about obsession and about dependency. Once I began to feel these things less, I begun to think I felt less love. It's not true. I used to feel that every step I took towards myself, every step I took away from my idolisation and dependency on Abigail, meant I loved her less. This also is not true. I do wonder, from time to time, what will happen to us, where we'll go. Whatever happens, though, she is really and truly (and finally) off the pedestal on which I so ill-advisedly placed her when we first met.

I have begun to recognise that the feelings which I had thought were true love, deeply spiritual, beyond normal human experience, were in fact clinging and overtly needy: embarrassing in retrospect. The difference now is that I no longer carry this experience as a personal failure. If anything, I am gladdened by it. It means I have moved on to a different plane, one of self-ownership and self-sufficiency. Eighteen months ago, I honestly thought, believed, *knew* for God's sake, that I couldn't live without her. Now I know I could. I also know I still don't want to. I used to dread her going out alone, as if leaving me for a few hours was synonymous with not loving me, abandoning me. Finding myself a more complete individual, the intensity of the need for someone else fades way. It was this need which I always misconstrued as love. Now I have to learn to love all over again. I've been reading Peck. He says that depression is a normal and healthy way of dealing with the giving up of such long held traits. So even my temporary depressions are okay. Is it me, or are things beginning to fall into place at long last? And in all of this, this understanding more about love and the nature of loving, I cannot forget Rachel's role in teaching me, in loving me. Even the smallest thought of her fills me with a warm indefinable sense of 'rightness'. I have been truly blessed to be able to count her as a friend.

There is something at work here, some outside force. It's as though the dominoes have started falling: the first one took me years to shift, sweating and toiling with little or no progress to show for it. Now, the impetus of the first collapse makes the next less onerous, until, before I know it, they begin to fall of their own accord; my pre-conceptions and sacred cows realising that they have no home within me any longer. It's a sort of anti-vicious circle, if such a thing exists: a virtuous cycle.

> *I am*
> *so powerful,*
> *I love*
> *so much,*
> *I feel*
> *infinity.*
> *Without me,*
> *nothing exists.*
> *I am love,*
> *and so*
> *are you.*

Wednesday 10th December

Evening. Late. I hear her now, turning over in bed, sleeping. I know that I love her and that she does love me. I believe that I am worthy of her love, as I know that she is worthy of mine. I know our future is out there. We talk about leaving Greece, maybe going to France. We are so right for each other, so much work, so much conscious effort, could not possibly be for nothing. I wrote once, after I had known her for only a few weeks,

"Have I met the mother of my children?" I was appalled at my presumption, the arrogance of my feelings.

Retsina takes effect
I see it in my scrawl
I feel it in my mood
I welcome its anaesthesia
One day
I'll realise
That the today I'm living
Is a success and a blessing.
Unhappy at times,
Dejected and scared,
But yet truly loved
And growing towards my goal.

Christmas approaches with gathering momentum. As another year ends, I can't help but feel that it is not an ending at all. It's a beginning. I started this diary two and half years ago. I think of the person I was then, and the person I am now. I think of the things which concerned me, the things I thought were important. I feel I'm a wise old sage looking at an impetuous adolescent, not judgmental, but understanding, and a little sad at the pain he has to go through to reach an understanding of his own. I am still very down on myself at times, but perhaps in relation to inappropriate yardsticks. When I consider the only true barometer of change, measuring my 'now' against my recent past, I do see how much progress I have made. If I were someone else, I would be proud of me. Don't I owe myself at least as much, if not more, than that fictional 'someone else'?

If I can't find compassion for myself, how can I expect anyone else to feel it for me? To be truly loveable, I think, we have to allow at least some self-compassion. I think that I have finally come to recognise that it exists within me. I begin to see myself as someone eminently worthwhile and worthy of love. Does that sound arrogant? It shouldn't. I am growing up. I am becoming the person whom I have always had the potential to be. About bloody time.

Telos.
Athens, December 1999

161

Characters and events are fictitious, oblique representations of a transfiguring episode. It is just possible that certain people recognise parts of themselves between these pages. All writing stems from experience; this is a work of fiction.

There are innumerable thanks to be offered. In no particular order, my thanks go to:

David and Terry, whose introductions to Greece will stay with me forever.

Anna, for reading this and for being so encouraging.

Stavroula, for teaching me the little Greek that remains with me and for being there.

Adrian, for leading me within.

Micha and Dagma, for getting me out in a moment of crisis, and without whom neither I nor this novel would exist.

Amy, who inspired more than she knows.

Dad, for the courage it takes to distance oneself...

www.scottlangston.org

www.ingramcontent.com/pod-product-compliance
Lightning Source LLC
Chambersburg PA
CBHW030514260626
47157CB00005B/1740